The Case of the Negligent Nymph

Erle Stanley Gardner

Mayflower

Granada Publishing Limited
Published in 1969 by Mayflower Books Ltd
Frogmore, St Albans, Herts AL2 2NF
Reprinted 1973

First published in Great Britain by
William Heinemann Ltd 1956
Copyright © Erle Stanley Gardner
Made and printed in Great Britain by
Hunt Barnard Printing Ltd
Aylesbury, Bucks.
Set in Intertype Plantin

"Looks?"
"Lots."
"Figure?"
"Swell."
Della Street said, "Well, boys will be boys."

Perry Mason was quietly canoeing past
the millionaire's island surveying the real
estate. A beautiful girl in a low-cut evening
gown dashed into the water and a ferocious
dog tore after her. Male pride got the better
of his lawyer's discretion.

Such a beautiful girl – such a grisly scene.

When Mason hauled her dripping and panting
into his canoe he became an accomplice in
crime. When he asked a few questions the
answer was: *murder.*

While writing *The Case of the Negligent Nymph* I was investigating two real-life murder cases, the bizarre ramifications of which rival any of the plots I have created in fiction.

Three outstanding criminologists have been associated with me in these investigations – Dr Le Moyne Snyder, physician and surgeon, attorney-at-law, internationally known criminologist; Raymond Schindler, the famous private detective, and the late Leonarde Keeler, whose sudden and unexpected death, news of which has just reached me, has been a great shock to all of us.

Some months ago, Harry Steeger, the editor and co-owner of *Argosy* Magazine, accompanied me on a trip down the wild, rugged peninsula of Baja, California. During the long evenings while the blaze of our camp-fires illuminated the weird branches of the *cardon* trees, we discussed two of the cases I had handled during my career as a lawyer where I had befriended penniless unfortunates who had been wrongfully convicted of crime.

Steeger told me that if I ever encountered any more such cases which I wished to investigate, *Argosy* Magazine would co-operate with us in every way.

I realised that the only way such a national magazine could help penniless persons who had been wrongfully convicted, yet had exhausted all their legal remedies, was by having a board of experts investigate such cases. It was, of course, necessary that the men composing such a board be of such stature in their profession that their opinions would carry the greatest weight.

I approached Dr Le Moyne Snyder, Leonarde Keeler and Raymond Schindler. These men promptly agreed to co-operate with us in every way.

To date, two cases have been fully investigated and duly reported in *Argosy* in a department that is called 'The Court of Last Resort'. In both of these cases the magazine was able to show that the men had been improperly convicted. In one case, the man had served thirteen years on a life sentence for murder. In the other, the man had been in the penitentiary for more than five years on a sentence of manslaughter.

Both men were released by the authorities.

It is a stupendous undertaking to reopen a case after it has finally been closed and the defendant has been convicted. There is, in fact, virtually no legal way in which this can be accomplished. We are forced to find clues the authorities overlooked, and convince the pardoning powers of the true facts. To re-examine reams of musty evidence, to try to run down stale clues on a cold trail means the expenditure of enormous effort, time and money. As cases continue to pour in, we find that our time is taxed to the limit trying to make even a preliminary appraisal in order to select the most worthy cases for investigation.

Yet there is the greatest satisfaction to be derived from this work and it has a thrill and excitement all its own.

While all of us are serving without compensation, *Argosy* has furnished the money to pay for transcripts, depositions, travelling expenses, etc.

The work has provided us with thrills a-plenty, and many the night we have paced the floor debating our best procedure, digging into huge volumes of printed transcript, debating the significance of clues which had been overlooked or misconstrued.

During the writing of this bok I have been literally 'up to my neck' in two other cases, one a case on the Pacific Coast, where I have been working with Raymond Schindler; the other a case in Michigan, where I have been working with Dr Snyder.

The case on the Pacific Coast involves two men charged with a first-degree murder for which the District Attorney refused to prosecute them on the ground that they had committed no crime. Yet, special prosecutors were appointed and the men were convicted, sentenced to death, the sentence commuted to life imprisonment, and the men have been in prison for some thirteen years.

In the Michigan case, Rabbi Joshua S. Sperka of Detroit consulted us about a penniless Jewish prisoner who had been in the Jackson penitentiary for seventeen years on a life sentence for murder. Our investigations, published in *Argosy*, caused the prosecutor to launch an independent investigation, as a result of which he has stated publicly he now believes the man was wrongfully convicted.

As I write this, the prosecutor has filed a petition in court asking that a new trial be granted this man and the entire case reopened, a move which is absolutely without precedent in the state's history.

And because I would like to make some public acknowledgment of my thanks and appreciation to these associates of mine who have made such sacrifices, to *Argosy* Magazine, to Harry Steeger, editor and co-owner, and Harold Goldsmith, his partner, I am dedicating this book to *Argosy's* 'Court of Last Resort', and to the men who have made it possible.

October, 1949   E. S. G.

CHAPTER ONE

From his rented canoe Perry Mason sized up the Alder estate as a general sizes up a prospective battlefield.

The moon, a few days past the full, made a shimmering path of silver in the east, and served to illuminate Mason's objective, an island connected with the mainland by a fifty-foot steel-and-concrete bridge.

On that island George S. Alder's huge two-storeyed mansion faced the narrow channel, as a castle might look down upon its protecting moat.

Fencing off the estate from the curious eyes of passers-by on the mainland was a brick wall topped with wrought iron and studded with broken glass. On the bay side were signs warning trespassers they would be prosecuted. A long wharf ran out into the sluggish waters, a sandspit on the northern side gave a crescent-shaped bathing beach and, behind that, a well-kept lawn became a velvety green carpet, thanks to the aid of loam which had been trucked in at great expense.

Alder's legal position seemed, at least on the surface, to be fully as impregnable as the island estate which isolated him and his wealth from the mainland. But Perry Mason was by no means an ordinary lawyer. It was never his policy to attack where the enemy expected the blow to fall. Rather, he preferred to devise some ingenious objective all his own. Hence his nocturnal survey of the place which meant more to Alder than all of the far-flung empire which he controlled.

On this particular evening Alder was entertaining, and, for the most part, his guests had evidently come from the two large, sea-going yachts which were riding at their moorings a quarter of a mile offshore. Two power launches, rich with polished mahogany, gleaming with burnished brass, were tied up at the private wharf of the Alder estate. And rumour had it that beams of invisible light guarded this wharf so that the moment any craft approached within ten feet an alarm sounded automatically, floodlights blazed into brilliance, and a powerful siren sent out its piercing scream.

Mason silently paddled his canoe close to the sandspit, studying the contours.

9

A hooded electric light was fastened to a board sign in such a manner that it illuminated the legend painted in red letters. These letters could be read a hundred and fifty feet away: PRIVATE PROPERTY. NO TRESPASSING—BEWARE OF VICIOUS DOGS WHICH WILL ATTACK TRESPASSERS ON SIGHT. KEEP OFF!

It was at this point in his survey that Mason suddenly became conscious of the swimmer.

Apparently the figure had not as yet seen the canoe, but was drifting along down the tide with slow, evenly timed, powerful strokes.

Mason, suddenly curious, held his canoe steady against the slowly ebbing tide and watched.

The figure landed on the sandspit within a few feet of the illuminated sign. Moonlight and the illumination from the sign were sufficient to show that the swimmer was a woman. She had apparently been swimming in the nude with a small waterproof sack tied to her back. From this sack she removed a bath towel with which she dried her slender, athletic body. Then she produced stockings, shoes, and a low-cut evening gown.

Fascinated, Mason shipped his dripping paddle into the rented canoe, took his night glasses from their case and raised the binoculars to his eyes.

He could see that she was blondish, good-looking and apparently completely assured.

She was not hurrying, nor was she loitering. She was as calmly unrushed as though she had been dressing at home in front of a mirror, and, once she had adjusted the sleeveless, strapless gown, she made up her face by the aid of a compact, using the light from the warning sign to guide her.

Having completed the make-up to her satisfaction, she left the waterproof bag on the ground, draped the wet bath towel over the support which held the light above the warning sign, and started walking towards the house, following a flagstone path which wound its way across the green of the lawn.

From the house came an occasional sound of isolated shrill women's laughter, the patter of voices, an occasional burst of general merriment.

Quite evidently the guests of George S. Alder were enjoying themselves, and it seemed equally evident that they had no reason to anticipate that an attractive guest who had arrived at the island by such surreptitious means was about to join them.

Fascinated, Mason watched through his binoculars, noticing

the young woman's smooth-hipped walk, her easy assurance as, with the long skirt of her gown draped over her arm, she calmly followed the flagstoned path until she was at length swallowed in the shadow of the house.

The lawyer sat in his canoe, binoculars ready, waiting. There was no slightest indication from the house that any untoward events were in the making.

For some fifteen minutes Mason sat watching and waiting, studying the house with his binoculars, from time to time thrusting the paddle into the water to hold the canoe against the tide while he awaited developments.

There was, of course, the possibility that this latest arrival was either an invited guest or someone who was sufficiently acquainted with the household to be certain of her welcome, but in either event she would hardly have left the waterproof bag and the towel there by the illuminated sign.

Mason glanced impatiently at the luminous dial of his wrist-watch. It was getting late, and he wanted to return the canoe and get back to town. He had surveyed the accretion line of the sandspit enough to form a definite plan of action. Within the next few days George S. Alder would be given a jolt which would cause him considerable inconvenience. Yet, at the moment, the lawyer dared not leave. He could not overlook the potential possibilities inherent in this surreptitious visitor who had appeared swimming out of the darkness with the deft stroke of one who is as much at home in the water as on land. Certainly there was something . . .

Suddenly Mason heard the barking of a dog. It was the excited, hysterical barking of an animal lunging against his chain.

Abruptly, lights flashed on in some of the back rooms of the Alder mansion. Mason heard shouting, the renewed barking of the dog.

Balancing himself in the canoe, the lawyer studied the house through his binoculars.

The figure of the young woman appeared at one of the windows. She slid over the sill and lowered herself. The long skirt momentarily caught on the window-sill, then she let go with her hands and, with a flutter of billowing skirts, dropped to the ground and started running.

First she ran towards one of the gates in the wall, then as the sound of shouting intensified in the house behind her, she veered back towards the water.

Through his binoculars, Mason could see men and women mil-

11

ling around in the room she had left so abruptly. Then he saw a man's form framed against the window, heard him shout.

The words were unintelligible, but there could be no mistaking the tone of the man's voice. It was a shout of discovery, and the tone was that which conveys understanding even to inarticulate, wild animals deeply hidden in brush, which at the sound of that note of triumphant discovery in the voice of the hunter automatically leap into startled flight.

The girl was running in a sheer panic now, coming straight towards the water, heedless of the towel and the white waterproof bag which she had left when she came ashore.

From a moment the man stood in the window, shouting, then he abruptly vanished.

The barking of the dog reached a shrill crescendo, then suddenly stopped.

Mason glanced from the running woman, who was sprinting directly towards his canoe, back to the window.

Suddenly he realised why the dog had stopped barking. The man had unchained him.

A dark streak of motion came hurtling through the window. For a moment, Mason's binoculars clearly showed the form of a Doberman pinscher as it sailed out in a great leap. Then the animal struck the ground and wasted a few precious seconds picking up the trail of the fugitive, following scent and running towards the gate.

All at once the dog saw the fleeing figure and in powerful surging leaps, he came bounding across the lawn.

The girl splashed into the water.

Mason could see that she was holding some object in her right hand. Her left hand grabbed up the folds of her skirt. She made four or five long, splashing jumps, then, falling headlong as the water deepened, started to swim.

The dog, running silently, reached the edge of the lawn, cleared the short strip of sandy beach, made a long, flying leap into the water, and started swimming.

He was close enough so that Mason could hear the little whining noises of eagerness in the animal's throat as it swam with shoulders high out of the water.

The frantic young woman had crossed the bow of Mason's canoe, apparently without seeing it. The dog, in deep water, was now less sure of himself.

Thrusting the blade of his paddle into the water, Mason shot

12

the canoe into the space between the girl and the pursuing dog. With the paddle he pushed the dog's shoulder, swinging him round so that the animal was pointed back towards the shore.

The dog gave a growling, angry bark, whirled and grabbed the blade of the paddle with his teeth, hung on.

Mason twisted the paddle, turning the dog over in the water, forcing him to let go his hold.

For a moment, with the water in his eyes, the dog was confused. Then he started swimming once more, powerfully, purposefully.

Again Mason pushed the dog completely around. Again the dog snapped at the blade of the paddle.

The young woman, now aware of what was going on, was using all her strength to put distance between herself and the dog.

The third time Mason pushed his paddle against the swimming animal. The dog once more grabbed the blade of the paddle. Once more, Mason twisted him over on his back, held him momentarily under water, and this time when the confused animal reached the surface he was swimming back towards the island.

Mason turned the canoe, sent it swiftly to the exhausted girl.

'Get in,' he said. 'Climb in over the bow so you don't upset us.'

She glanced over her shoulder to look at him, a swift, desperate appraisal. Then, as though realising she had no other alternative, she raised her right hand, dropped something into the bow of the canoe. Then, catching hold of the bow with two hands, one on each side, she suddenly raised herself with a powerful thrust of strong young arms, and came over the bow, sliding along to lie momentarily flat on her stomach, kicking her legs clear of the water. Then she rolled over with a swift, lithe motion, doubled her knees in under her, pulled down her wet dress and said gaspingly, 'I don't know . . . who you are . . . but you'd better paddle like hell!'

Flashlights, flickering like fireflies, appeared on the shore, and Mason heard someone shout, 'There she is! She's swimming.'

After a second or two, another voice said, 'No, it's the dog. He's coming back!'

The flashlights momentarily converged on the dog, then raised, and questing beams circled out over the dark waters.

One of the more powerful flashlights caught the canoe. Mason promptly ceased paddling, kept his back turned, his face down, and said to the girl, 'Better keep your head down.'

'I know,' she said, her head lowered. 'Damn these low neck-lines. I *would* have to be betrayed by the styles . . . I feel as prominent as a silk hat at snowballing time . . . Wish I had something that would cover up these shoulders.'

A man's voice from the shore shouted, 'There's a boat out there. That's a boat, I tell you!'

For a few moments the flashlight held the canoe, then lost it, and circled blindly as the searchers failed to make allowance for the drifting tide.

Mason used the paddle once more, sending the canoe out farther from the shore and down the bay, speeding along on the tide.

'Well?' he asked, at length.

She said, 'Thanks for the buggy ride. Only it's a canoe.'

'I'm afraid,' Mason told her, 'it's going to take a little more than that.'

'To do what?'

'To square things.'

'What things?'

'My conscience, for one.'

'What's the matter with your conscience? Is it unusually tender?'

'No. Only usually tender.'

She said, 'Let me get my breath and I'll tell you all about it.'

'Where do you want to go?'

'Out to my yacht. It's a little job, the *Kathy-Kay*, and I'll have to get my bearings to . . .'

Mason said, 'We'll stay here on neutral territory until we know what the situation is. I acted on impulse. The sight of that dog dashing after you with bared fangs speeded my generous impulses.'

'What do you want to know?'

'Who you are, what you were after.'

'Oh, I see. You're willing to be a dashing knight, but you also want to be a careful knight.'

'Exactly.'

'After all, you know, I'm an international gem thief and those are the dowager's jewels I just tossed in the bottom of the canoe.'

'Intended as a joke,' Mason said, 'but since it was your idea, we'll investigate it.'

'Oh, all right,' she said. 'I'll tell you, but give me a few seconds to catch my breath.' She remembered to exaggerate her breathlessness while she fought for time.

'And give you a chance to think up a story?' Mason asked.

'Don't be silly. You should try running from a vicious dog. I felt like the mechanical rabbit in a dog race.'

14

'And moved just about as fast,' Mason said.

'The water saved me,' she admitted. 'And you with your providential canoe. How did *you* happen to be there?'

Mason grinned. 'Let me (puff, puff) get my breath, and then I'll (puff, puff) tell you all about it.'

She laughed, squirmed round to a more comfortable position, and sized him up.

The moonlight fell on her face, and Mason saw young symmetrical features, deep brown eyes, high cheek-bones, a short nose, a full-lipped but small mouth, and a figure clothed in clinging wet garments which outlined it admirably.

She said frankly, 'I feel naked. One doesn't wear much under these dresses, and it certainly clings, doesn't it?'

'Any time,' he told her.

'Any time, what?'

'That you have recovered your breath, you may tell me about your loot.'

'Oh, that,' she said. 'Sit tight and don't be frightened. I'm accustomed to canoes. I won't tip it over.'

She swung quickly, moving with such a sure sense of balance that the canoe hardly swayed. She reached into the bow, raised an object which glistened in the moonlight, and extended it to the lawyer. '*There* are the dowager's diamonds,' she said.

The object was a plain glass bottle carefully stoppered, roughened on one side as though half of the bottle had been made from ground glass. On the inside was something white, not a liquid, but what seemed to be a piece of tightly rolled paper.

Mason shook the bottle, then held it up so that he could better inspect it in the moonlight.

'The jewels,' the girl said dryly. 'I suppose now I can count on being turned over to the police.'

'What the deuce *is* this?' Mason asked.

'It's a bottle with a piece of paper in it.'

Mason put down the bottle to study the girl more carefully. 'And is there perhaps,' he asked, 'some other trinket that goes with it? Perhaps a diamond ring or a watch or something?'

'Concealed on my person?' she asked, indicating the lines of her wet dress. 'In this outfit, Mr Inquisitor? I couldn't smuggle a postage stamp, let alone a rhinestone.'

From the direction of the wharf came the sputtering sound of a motor, then a choking back-fire, followed by a sudden roar of staccato explosions.

15

'Oh,' she exclaimed in dismay, 'they've got one of the speed-boats going. Quick! To those yachts over there. Give it everything you have. We can't let them catch us here.'

Where a moment before she had been triumphantly sure of herself, inclined to engage in banter, she was now in a panic of desperation.

Mason hesitated a moment, then sank the paddle deep into the water.

'Don't think this thing is going to be terminated when we get to your yacht,' Mason said. 'I'm going to continue this investigation!'

'Continue anything you want to,' she said, 'but let's not be caught here like a couple of saps. They have a searchlight on that motorboat and . . . We'll never make it!'

Aboard the speedboat, a canvas cover was jerked off the searchlight and a long, wicked pencil of light started swinging back and forth across the dark space of the water.

'Faster, faster!' she said, looking apprehensively back over her shoulder. 'They're too far upstream. If we can *only* make it. Another hundred yards and we'll be . . .'

The searchlight suddenly, as though drawn by a magnet, swung in a half circle, passed directly over the canoe, hesitated a moment, wavered back, then speared the occupants in white glare.

'Oh, they've found us!' the girl exclaimed. 'Please, *please* paddle.'

The motorboat swung in a half circle, bore down upon them at speed.

A yacht anchored broadside became interposed between the speedboat and the canoe, momentarily blotting out the beam of the searchlight.

'Hold everything,' Mason said, swinging the canoe abruptly towards the anchored yacht. 'Grab something so you can hang on.'

'No, no,' she said, 'this isn't the one. We can't go aboard this, and . . .'

'Grab,' Mason commanded.

She caught hold of a porthole, swinging the canoe abruptly around.

'Now duck,' Mason ordered, as the canoe came in close to the yacht.

Suddenly the girl sensed his manoeuvre and pulled the canoe forward as she dropped to the bottom. Mason, completely reversing his direction, paddled back under the bow of the yacht and up the other side. The speedboat in the meantime had swung wide so that the beam of the spotlight could pick up the canoe again on the yacht's port side. Mason waited until the momentum of the speedboat had carried it past, then paddled out from the starboard side of the yacht.

Waves made by the speedboat hit the canoe head-on, threatened for a moment to capsize it, then subsided. Mason crossed the wake of the speedboat, which by this time was slewing in a scrambled turn, having quite apparently put on too much speed considering the proximity of anchored yachts.

The girl cautiously surveyed the various yachts riding at anchor, and said, 'The one we want is that little one a hundred yards over there. Here they are, coming back to look for us.'

Mason sized up the situation. 'Sit tight. I'm going to try to make it to that big yacht over there.'

'But that belongs to . . .'

'We're just going to use it as a shield,' he explained. 'They've lost us now, and if we can keep out of sight they *may* think we went aboard one of these larger yachts.'

Mason put everything he had into paddling across the dark stretch of water. The speedboat made a complete circle but, by the time the searchlight had a clean sweep over open water, Mason had gained the far side of the yacht, checked the progress of the canoe, and swung in to the protecting shadows of the yacht's hull. As the speedboat made another wide circle, Mason slipped under the bow of the yacht and came back on the starboard side. Watching his opportunity, he rounded the stern and paddled swiftly to another good-sized yacht which had enough freeboard to offer them complete protection.

By this time the girl was trembling with excitement and the chill of her wet clothes.

Mason, checking the progress of the canoe in the shelter of the third yacht, could feel the faint vibrations of her shivers as her hands gripped the sides of the light canoe.

'You're cold,' he said. 'You're shivering.'

'Of course I'm cold! These clothes have become icy, but don't let a little shivering bother you. You're doing fine. Now if you can only work down towards that little yacht . . .'

She broke off with chattering teeth.

Mason said, 'You'll catch cold. You shouldn't . . .'

'What do you want me to do, take it off? she asked.

'You might as well,' Mason told her.

17

'I might at that,' she admitted, pulling the wet garment away from the skin. 'It clings, and sticks, and I suppose it's darn near transparent. But . . .'

'Oh, oh!' Mason interrupted, 'they're making a wide circle completely around the outside of the anchorage. Perhaps we can make it. Want to take a chance?'

She said sarcastically, 'You should know by this time that I'm a conservative young woman who *never* takes a chance.'

Mason shot the canoe out from the protection of the yacht, across a strip of open water, then gained the side of the little yacht the girl had pointed out.

'Quick,' she said, scrambling abroad. 'We're going to have to do something with this canoe. That's why they're circling, looking for the yacht which has . . .'

'Hoist it aboard,' Mason told her.

'There isn't room to put it anywhere on deck.'

'Slide it into the cabin,' Mason suggested. 'Put part of it in the cabin and leave part of it down here . . .'

'All right. Can we lift it?'

'Sure. It's an aluminium canoe. You take the bow, I'll take the stern. All right, let's go.'

They lifted the dripping canoe across the deck, and opening the cabin door, slid part of the bow into the cabin.

'Now,' she said, 'I'm going to have a drink of whisky and you're going to have a drink of whisky. Then you're going to be a gentleman and turn your back. I can't close the doors of the cabin with the canoe in there and there's enough moonlight so . . .'

Mason said, 'I'll go outside and keep an eye on that speedboat . . .'

'You most certainly will do nothing of the sort. They'll see you. You won't be able to resist sticking your head up over the side just when they happen to swing the searchlight. You stay right here.'

Mason said, 'I want some assurance that this bottle was the only thing you took. I . . .'

She said, 'Sit tight and I'll throw you my wet clothes. You can search them. I wish you wouldn't be so darned suspicious.'

'I know,' Mason told her. 'I'm a narrow-minded old fuddy-duddy. I've always been suspicious whenever I see a woman jumping out of a window . . .'

'So you saw that, did you?'

He nodded.

She said, 'Keep your eyes closed. Here comes a very wet and soggy dinner dress. Then I'm going to slip into a housecoat and . . . If I can find the darn thing . . . Here it is . . . Now, wait a minute . . . Okay, now you may open your eyes and we're going to have a great big jolt of whisky without water and without ice.'

'Make mine light,' Mason warned.

Mason heard the clink of glasses, saw her moving about the small cabin, then heard the splash of liquid, and a glass was thrust into his hand.

'I think this calls for a toast. Here's to crime,' she said and then laughed.

Mason sipped the whisky, heard her pour herself a second drink.

'Ready for a refill ?'

'No, I'm doing fine. Don't hit that too hard.'

'I won't,' she promised. 'I don't ordinarily take much, but I'm chilled right through to the bone.'

Mason said, 'Suppose we take an inventory.'

'Of what ?'

'That bottle.'

'You saw it.'

'I want to see what's inside of it.'

She said, 'Now look, you've been a good scout, you were really a friend in need and I'm terribly grateful. Sometime tomorrow I'll dress to the teeth, get in touch with you and tell you how grateful I really am. In the meantime . . .'

'In the meantime,' Mason said, 'I'm an attorney. I have a position to uphold. So far as I'm concerned you're a housebreaker. Unless you can satisfy me that you weren't stealing I'm going to have to turn you over to the police.'

'The police!'

'That's right.'

She hesitated a moment, then said, 'And you're an attorney ?'

'Yes.'

'Then perhaps you can help . . . Listen!'

The speedboat came roaring close to the yacht. Waves rocked the light craft in a series of quick rolls.

An exasperated voice from the deck of one of the other yachts yelled. 'Get that speedboat out of this yacht anchorage, you drunken fools.'

A voice from the speedboat shouted, 'We're chasing a thief. Have you seen a boat with two people in it ?'

'Haven't seen a thing,' the voice on the yacht said wearily. 'Why don't you go home and go to bed?'

The speedboat swept around in another turn, then the motor slowed, apparently while the occupants held a conference. After a few moments the motor speeded up once more. The boat turned back and the sound of the motor diminished in the distance.

The girl sighed. 'Thank heavens they're going back.'

'Going back to notify the police,' Mason said.

'Well,' she announced hopefully, 'while they're doing that you could . . . We could get the canoe out and . . .'

'Yes,' Mason said dryly, '*you* could go on about *your* business. I'd be out in the bay paddling a canoe. Before I could get back to where I'm going I might be picked up and questioned – and just what would you suggest I tell them?'

She said, 'This is purely a personal and a private matter.'

'And once the police enter into it, it becomes a purely impersonal and public matter. I have no desire to be charged as being an accessory after the fact.'

She said, 'Let's take blankets off the berths and put them up over the portholes so we can use a small flashlight. We'll take a look at it together.'

'Fair enough,' Mason said. 'Only our friends won't be idle while we're doing all that.'

'No, I suppose not, but they haven't any lead to this yacht.'

'Not so long as we're aboard,' Mason explained patiently. 'I've already pointed out that if I should be picked up before I reached shore, I'd have to explain where I'd been and what I'd been doing and . . .'

'Well,' she said in dismay, 'you can't stay *here* all night.'

She thought that over for a minute; then, before Mason could say anything, added hastily, 'Yes, you can too. You'll have to. It's the *only* thing to do. We're going to have to keep that darn canoe in the cabin so it will be out of sight, and then along in the morning we'll very casually start out on a fishing trip with you attired in sports clothes, sitting up in the trolling chair with a fishing rod and . . .'

'In the meantime,' Mason said, 'let's start putting blankets over the portholes, because I'm going to take a good look at that bottle.'

She hesitated, then said, 'All right. It's a deal.'

Mason had vague glimpses of her moving around in the cabin, heard the sound of woollen blankets being shaken. Then on the port side, moonlight was suddenly blotted out. A few seconds later moonlight on the starboard side vanished into darkness.

'Now, then,' the girl said, and the beam of the flashlight penetrated the darkness.

Her voice was quavering with excitement. She said, "We can keep the light from the flashlight down close to the floor and it'll be . . . Where's that bottle?'

'In the canoe, I believe,' Mason said.

She cupped her hands over the lens of the flashlight, funnelling the light through a small opening.

The light shining through her skin showed her fingers outlined in blood red, also showed well-browned legs through the opening in the skirt of the housecoat.

Then she said. 'Here it is,' and leaning forward, removed one hand from the flashlight.

Mason's hands closed about the bottle before the girl could reach it. 'I'll hold the bottle, you hold the flashlight.'

'You're *so* good to me,' she murmured sarcastically.

Mason inspected the bottle, said, 'It's going to take a pair of tweezers to get this paper out. It's been rolled, thrust in the neck of the bottle, and then has expanded.'

'How about some long-nosed pliers,' she said. 'I have those handy in a tool kit and . . .'

'Let's try them. They should work.'

For a moment Mason was in darkness as the beam of the flashlight was turned towards the bow of the cabin. Then he heard a drawer open, heard the sould of metal against metal, and a moment later she was back with the flashlight and a pair of long-nosed pliers.

Mason inserted the long slender jaws in the neck of the bottle, started twisting the paper around and around, and at the same time gently drawing it towards the narrow mouth of the bottle, until finally he had it twisted in a spiral so that he was able to work it out without tearing it.

It then became apparent that there were several sheets of paper, all bearing an identical embossed heading: ON BOARD YACHT THAYERBELLE. GEORGE S. ALDER, *Owner*.

Mason held the document pressed against his knee and the two of them read the firm, clear handwriting together:

Somewhere off Catalina Island. I, Minerva Danby, make this statement because if anything should happen to me I want justice done.

I am writing this on the yacht of George S. Alder, the *Thayerbelle*.

21

Because I have information which will in all probability deprive George Alder of much of his fortune, he may do *anything* to seal my lips.

I'm afraid I have been careless, not to say stupid.

When George Alder's father died, he left all the stock of the huge corporation known as Alder Associates, Inc. in a trust, one part to his stepdaughter, Corrine Lansing, one part to his son, George S. Alder. The survivor was to take all the stock. A brother of the father, Dorley H. Alder, was to have the *voting power* of one-third of the stock and a guaranteed income for life, but he was to have no interest in the trust unless both of the younger people died before he did. Dividends were to be paid on a basis of one-third to each. There were, however, ten shares of stock which were not in the trust, stock held by Carmen Monterrey. I set these things down in writing to show that I appreciate the danger I am in and the reason for it.

Corrine Lansing went to South America. She had been suffering from a nervous condition, which became steadily worse.

I met her on an aeroplane while I was flying over the Andes between Santiago, Chile, and Buenos Aires in the Argentine. She was terribly nervous and distraught and I tried to steady her down a bit. As a result she took a sudden liking to me and insisted that I should start travelling with her, sharing accommodations but entirely at her expense.

Because I was travelling on a very limited budget, and because I thought I could perhaps do her some good, and without knowing anything at all about her or her background, I accepted.

Corrine had her maid with her, Carmen Monterrey, who had been in the family for years and who, I gathered, had been a favourite of Corrine's stepfather.

Gradually I learned from her the family background, about her brother and the terms of her father's will. Carmen Monterrey, of course, knew all about it also. She was treated as 'one of the family' and Corrine Lansing never hesitated to discuss business matters in her presence.

Despite the fact that the arrangement was very advantageous to me from a financial standpoint, the time came when I simply couldn't put up with it any longer. Day by day, Corrine Lansing became progressively worse. I had reason to believe she was completely unbalanced on some things. Carmen told me Corrine had threatened to kill me if I should try to leave her.

Under the circumstances, I feared to have an open break lest she might become violent. In short, the woman had developed a fierce, passionate attachment for me and insisted that I be near her all the time. It was quite apparent that she was rapidly becoming a mental case. She wanted to monopolise me. There was a definite desire to dominate, which not only annoyed but frightened me. It seems she had a well-developed persecution complex and had decided someone was trying to poison her and that having me constantly with her was her only protection.

I felt sorry for her, but I began to feel afraid for myself and I know Carmen Monterrey was equally afraid.

It happened that events made it necessary for George Alder to fly to South America, bringing some papers for Corrine to sign, and on the day he was due to arrive and while she was at the beauty parlour I packed my bags and left a note for her saying I had been unexpectedly called back home by a telegram informing me a close relative was very ill and not expected to live. Anticipating that she would go to the beauty parlour before meeting her half brother, I had previously reserved passage on a Pan American aeroplane flying north.

I fancied myself well free of an embarrassing entanglement and thought no more about it for weeks after my return. Then I read in the papers that Corrine was supposed to be dead, that she had disappeared on the afternoon of the day I had left her and no one had ever been able to find so much as a trace of her.

For a while it had been assumed she had merely wandered off in a fit of despondency. She had, it seemed, been much upset by the departure of a 'friend', and it was feared had gone to look for her. With the passage of time it was assumed she must have met with some fatal accident.

Detectives were employed and searched without getting any tangible results. It was, however, definitely established that the woman was mentally unbalanced at the time of her disappearance

Naturally, upon reading this, I went to George S. Alder and told him what I knew and offered to help in any way I could. I felt conscience-stricken because I knew Corrine had gone to search for me when she disappeared.

Alder was at first very grateful, and then became friendly, and I am frank to admit that I was foolish enough to feel that perhaps there was something more to his friendship than just a desire to see that the evidence concerning his sister's death was properly established.

I had told George Alder I would take a cruise with him and had been looking forward to it with a great deal of pleasure. However, just before we embarked upon this cruise, I had occasion to go to the mental hospital at Los Merritos. I was leaving when in the yard I saw a woman whom I first thought to be a ghost.

It was Corrine Lansing!

I stood staring at her as though transfixed, and she looked at me with that peculiar gleam of an insane person in her eyes, but nevertheless she recognised me. She said, 'Minerva! What are you doing here? Minerva, *Minerva*, *Minerva*!' and started screaming until an attendant rushed to her and told her she mustn't excite herself. By that time, Corrine was hysterical and violent, and she was rushed to a room where she could be treated.

By discreet inquiries I learned that this woman had been picked up on the streets of Los Angeles, wandering as in a dream. She seemed to know nothing about herself and had never been able to give a name, or the names of any relatives. At times she would claim to be one person, at times another, each time giving a different name. Then at times she could remember no name to give, but would sit helpless and distraught.

Very much upset and completely unnerved, I hastened to find George Alder so I could tell him what I had found.

George Alder was not aboard the yacht when I arrived, and no one seemed to know where he was. I waited for him to return, but, when he had not come aboard by ten o'clock, I left word that he was to call me, and went to my cabin to wait.

I had had a fatiguing day. I stretched out on the couch and was soon asleep. I was awakened from that sleep by the sound of the engines and, from the motion of the yacht, realised we were at sea and that there was a heavy sea running. Moreover, the wind was howling about the yacht so that I knew a sudden storm had descended upon us.

I rang for the steward and asked him, despite the lateness of the hour, to get in touch with George Alder, and tell him I must see him at once.

George sent back word that a sudden terrific windstorm had descended upon us and that he was busy with the yacht, but would come just as soon as he could. It was just an hour ago, at two o'clock in the morning, that George came to my cabin.

I told him what had transpired. He asked me several shrewd questions, and then asked me several times whether I had repeated what had happened to anyone.

At the time I was too stupid to realise what he had in mind. I was rather proud of my reticence in keeping my own counsel until I could bring the news to George Alder because I knew how he disliked newspaper notoriety.

I am now trying to make allowances for the fact that I have had a very trying experience, that the events of the last twenty-four hours have been such as to shock me greatly. But, despite all of my attempts to discount what has happened and account for it as being nerves, I am filled with apprehension.

George Alder sat in my cabin after I had told him my story and looked at me with steady, appraising eyes.

I began to feel uneasy. It was as though a snake were trying to charm a bird.

'You're sure you haven't told anyone, Minerva?' he asked.

'Not a soul,' I said. 'You can trust my sense of discretion on that.'

And then suddenly I saw in his eyes that same look which I had seen in the eyes of his sister, the look of an insane person contemplating some peculiarly cunning means of attaining an end. He arose without a word, turned towards the door, paused in the doorway, fumbled with the lock for a moment, gave me once more that queer look, and then went out and slammed the door behind him.

I suddenly felt myself filled with apprehension. I wanted to be put ashore. I wanted to communicate with someone. I ran to the door.

It was locked. George had locked it from the outside as he went out.

I flung myself against the door and pounded with my fists. I kicked. I pulled at the knob and I screamed.

Nothing happened. The noise of the storm was howling about the yacht. The hull was creaking and groaning with the strains and stresses set up by the huge waves. Wind shrieked through the rigging. The crashing waves made my screams seem weak and puny.

I have repeatedly tried ringing for the steward. Nothing happens. I have tried telephoning. The line is dead. I realise now that George has cut the wires leading from my cabin.

I have looked around, trying to find some means of communicating my predicament, some way of reaching someone, but the noise of the storm, the lateness of the hour, and the fact that I am isolated in a rear guest cabin has made this impossible.

I have one hope, and one hope alone. I have decided to write down everything that happened, seal it in a bottle, and toss that bottle out through the porthole. Then, if George should come back, I will tell him what I have done. I will tell him that the bottle will eventually drift ashore, and will most surely be found. In that way – well, at least I can *hope* that he will listen to reason, but I feel that the man, with the insane cunning which is apparently a family taint, intends to see to it that my lips will be for ever sealed.

(Signed) MINERVA DANBY

Mason felt the girl's fingers pressing into his arm. 'I've got him!' she exclaimed triumphantly. 'I've got him, I've got him, I've got him! Do you realise what this letter means ? I've got him!'

'It's me you're getting,' Mason pointed out. 'I may want to use that arm again.'

'Oh, I'm sorry.'

'Just who is this Minerva Danby ?' Mason asked.

'I don't know very much about her except what's in this letter. All I know is that she was drowned. She was washed overboard from Alder's yacht about six months ago. That was the story.'

Mason said cautiously, 'Since I now seem to have become an accessory after the fact to a full-scale burglary, you *might* tell me a little something about what happened.'

She said excitedly, 'Oh, I always knew that there was something fishy with this business about Corinne. I felt certain she wasn't dead, and now ... Oh, you can see what a terrific difference it makes.'

'Just what difference *does* it make ?'

She said, 'I'm related to Corrine, probably the only living blood relative she has. Oh, this is going to make a difference, a *big* difference.'

Mason said, 'Under the circumstances you'd better tell me a lot more.'

'What more is there to tell ? The letter speaks for itself.'

'It doesn't speak for you.'

'Why should *I* speak ?' she demanded.

Mason said, 'Let's try being practical for a change. I'm a responsible citizen. I find you committing burglary and circumstances conspire to put me in a position of helping you out.'

'You said you were a lawyer.'

'All right, I'm a lawyer. It just might be that George S. Alder would very much enjoy being in a position to accuse me of having conspired with you to steal this evidence from his house.'

'Can't you see,' she said, scornfully, 'that Alder can't accuse anyone of anything ? He doesn't *dare* let this letter be made public.'

'All right,' Mason said patiently. 'What are *you* going to do with the letter?'

'I'll make it public.'

'And just how will you then account for the fact that this letter came into your possession?'

'Why, I'll go to the newspapers. I'll say that . . .'

'Yes, go on,' Mason said.

'Couldn't I say that I found the letter?'

'Where?'

'On the beach somewhere.'

'And then Alder would introduce witnesses showing that the letter had been in his possession, that it had been taken from his house, and you'd be facing a perjury charge as well as a burglary charge.'

There was dismay in her voice. 'I hadn't thought of that.'

'I was satisfied you hadn't. Now suppose you tell me who you are, how you knew the letter was there, and a few other things.'

'And suppose I don't?'

'There's always the police.'

'*You* haven't told me anything about *you*,' she flared.

'That's right,' Mason said dryly, 'I haven't.'

She thought the situation over for several seconds, then said with sullen reluctance, 'I'm Dorothy Fenner. I have a job as secretary to a broker. When my mother died she left me a little money. I came here from Colorado two years ago.

'My mother was a sister of Cora Lansing. Cora married Jack Lansing. They had one child, Corrine. The marriage wasn't a success. Cora Lansing married Samuel Nathan Alder. They had one son, George S. Alder. Corrine is five years older than George.

'So you see that, despite the difference in ages, I'm Corinne's full cousin. We were very close. Aunt Cora died ten years ago, then George's father died and left the property in a sort of trust to Corrine, George and Dorley Alder, George's uncle.'

'How do you get along with the Alders?' Mason asked. 'Not very well, I take it.'

'I get along fine with Uncle Dorley. He's a splendid man. I don't get along with George Alder at all. No one does unless they let George dominate body and soul.'

'And how did you know about this letter?' Mason asked.

'I . . . I can't tell.'

'Better get your story ready,' Mason warned.

She said, 'I heard about it.'

'How?'

'Well, if you want to know, Uncle Dorley gave me the hint.'

'Indeed,' Mason said, his voice showing interest.

'It was just a question he asked,' she said. 'He told me he understood Pete Cadiz had picked up a letter Minerva Danby had written before she was washed overboard. He asked me if I knew anything about it; if George had said anything to me.'

'Do you know Pete Cadiz?'

'Sure. I guess all the yachtsmen know him. He's a sort of beachcomber. Everyone knows who he is.'

'Then Dorley knows about the letter?'

'He knows something about it.'

'And why didn't you go to George Alder and ask him about it point-blank?'

She said, 'That shows how little you know George Alder. I think he was ready to destroy this letter. He'd have done it already, if perhaps he didn't think Pete Cadiz or someone else knew what was in it.

'All I wanted to do was to read it. I knew George Alder was having a big party tonight and I know his house pretty well. I thought I could get in there while the guests were at dinner, go to George's study, get the bottle from his desk, read the letter, and see what was in it.

'You probably wouldn't know it, but he has the place trapped with all sorts of burglar alarms. There's only one way to get into the house without being detected. That's the way I used. I walked up to the point above the sandspit, undressed, put my clothes on my back and swam down to the island. I wore a dinner dress because if any of the servants had seen me, they'd have taken it for granted George had invited me as one of the guests.'

'You know the servants?'

'Of course.'

'How about the dog? You didn't seem to know him.'

'The dog double-crossed me,' she said bitterly. 'There must be some instinct that enabled him to know I was taking something that didn't belong to me. He was trained as a war dog and never got over it, and never will. Corrine picked him up after the Army finished with him. Carmen trained and fed him, and he loved her, but George took him over after Corrine's disappearance.'

'Do you have a camera aboard?'

'No, why?'

'I want to photograph this document.'

She said, 'I have a portable typewriter. We could copy it – but why do you want a copy when we have the original?'

'*You* have the original,' Mason said. 'In case *I* should ever be called upon to tell *my* story, I want to be sure that I tell it right. Now then, you're going to get out your portable typewriter, copy that letter, keep one copy for yourself and give me one copy.'

'And what do I do with the letter itself?'..

'Return it to George Alder, together with your apologies.'

'Are you crazy?'

Mason said, 'Think it over. You make a copy of the letter. You and I compare the copy with the original. Then you take the letter back to Alder, smile very sweetly and tell him that you just wanted to read it, but in the excitement you carried it away with you. Then you ask him what he intends to do about that letter.'

There was a long silence while she thought that over. 'Say,' she said at length, her voice suddenly enthusiastic, 'I guess you're not so dumb, after all.'

'Thank you,' Mason said fervently. 'I was beginning to have doubts.'

CHAPTER TWO

The canoe slid noiselessly down into the water.

Dorothy Fenner said in a low voice, 'Thanks for everything.'

'Don't mention it,' Mason told her.

'I wish I knew who you were.'

'Why?'

'It would make me feel safer. You don't know George S. Alder?'

Mason said, 'All you need to do is give him back that bottle and tell him a witness has seen the letter and has a copy.'

She said dubiously, 'It's easy for you to say. You don't know him.'

'Are you going to do it?'

'I don't know. I'll think it over. I think perhaps if I keep the original letter I may have more of a hold over him.'

'I'd advise you to read the law on blackmail,' Mason said. 'However, I haven't time to argue with you now. I'm hoping I can get to shore without being detected. Good night, Dorothy.'

'Good night, Mr Mysterious Whoever You Are, I like you – will you show up as a witness – in case I need you?'

'One never knows,' Mason said, and shoved off.

Mason leaned on the paddle and started for the lights on the landing at the canoe club.

The sound of a heavy-duty motor transmitted by the layer of damp air immediately over the water sounded increasingly and ominously louder, a ka-*pooog* . . . ka-*pooog* . . . ka-*pooog* . . . ka-*pooog*.

Mason gave the paddle everything he had. The light canoe, barely skimming the surface of the water, hissed swiftly towards the landing.

The canoe had been rented for the evening, the rental paid in advance, so Mason had only to tie it up at the float and walk away.

To his surprise there were no special officers on duty at the landing, and beyond the ominous sound of the heavy-duty motor, he had seemed to have the bay all to himself.

Now he hurried along the landing float, his hat pulled well down, the brim depressed, and walked rapidly to the place where he had left his car.

Della Street, Perry Mason's confidential secretary, was sitting in his car listening to the radio. She looked up and smiled as Mason opened the car door. She switched off the radio and said, 'You must have had quite a trip.'

'You get the telephoning done?' Mason asked.

'Everything,' she said. 'Then I came back here to wait. I've been here for nearly two hours.'

'I had an adventure,' Mason confessed.

'Didn't hear anything of the burglary, did you?'

'What burglary?'

'Our friend George S. Alder's house was robbed of fifty thousand dollars in jewellery.'

'The devil!' Mason exclaimed.

She laughed. 'I thought perhaps you might have been in on it.'

Mason's voice was filled with chagrin. 'I guess perhaps I was.'

She looked at him quizzically. 'Give.'

'You first,' he told her.

'All I know is what I heard over the radio a few minutes ago. A daring female burglar evidently swam or waded ashore from a light boat which had ferried her to the island and was waiting in the darkness for her. Dressed in a dinner gown, the servants took

29

her for one of the dinner guests. She was detected only by accident as she was rifling the man's desk. She jumped out of a window, ran to the water's edge, then jumped in, clothes and all, and started swimming. She was picked up by her accomplice and managed to make good her escape. Police have reason to believe she may have sought concealment on one of the yachts anchored somewhere in the bay. Police are going to throw out a cordon, and they're already establishing road blocks.'

'Just when did you hear all this?'

'It came over the radio about fifteen minutes ago. I was a little worried. I thought perhaps you might have tangled up with these people and – well, you know, evidently they were desperate.'

'Any clues?' Mason asked.

'The police have found a towel and a bathing cap, which the young woman left on the island – also a waterproof bag.'

Mason started the motor, switched on the headlights, backed the car out of the parking place, gunned the motor into life and rapidly shifted gears.

'Well,' Della Street said, 'you seem to be taking it quite seriously. What's the matter?'

'Believe it or not,' Mason said, '*I* was the male accomplice who showed up with the means of escape.'

'*You* were!'

'That's right. She made the getaway in my canoe.'

She looked at him for a moment, then suddenly laughed. 'I suppose,' she said, 'the purpose of this gag is to keep me awake during the drive back to town.'

'The purpose of the statement, which you erroneously call a gag, is to point out that a man should never act impulsively when encountering a strange woman.'

'You encountered her?'

'Yes.'

'Where?'

'Splashing out from the island in a very thin dinner dress, and not much else, a savage dog in hot pursuit.'

'And what did you do?'

'I acted on impulse and told her to get into the canoe.'

'Well,' Della Street said, 'I can appreciate the impulse, but at least you should have made her kick through with half of the jewellery.'

'She didn't take any jewellery,' Mason said. 'She took a piece of evidence, but the man in the case is too smart to be caught on anything like that, so he's claiming that he lost fifty thousand dollars in jewellery. And you can see where that leaves me.'

'How do you know she didn't take jewellery?'

'She – well, she took off her clothes and let me search the dress.'

'In the canoe?'

'No, aboard a yacht which she *said* was hers.'

'She stripped in front of . . . ?'

'It was dark. She undressed and tossed me the dress.'

'And that's the only way you know she didn't take the jewellery?'

'I'm afraid it is.'

Della Street made little tongue noises against the roof of her mouth. 'You should keep me with you – even if just for the purpose of searching women.'

'Damned if I shouldn't,' Mason said fervently.

'Did you find out anything about Alder?' Della Street asked.

Mason chuckled and said, 'Now *there* I believe I have something.'

'What?'

Mason said, 'Alder bought that island and paid a fabulous price for it. He wants to have a feudal castle all his own. He's that type. If anything should happen so that he couldn't control every square inch of that island, I think he'd go crazy.'

'But doesn't he own it all?'

'He owns it,' Mason said, 'but when they dredged the channel they put up a retaining wall and dumped soil against it. That formed the long, semicircular sandspit which projects out to the north-east.'

Della Street laughed and said, 'Of course I'm practising law by ear, but doesn't property formed by accretion belong to the owner of the adjacent soil?'

'Sure it does when the accretion is the result of *natural* causes; but I think there's a Supreme Court decision somewhere holding that property formed because of governmental activities such as dredging in a channel is government property. Now if that's the case and someone should squat on the sandspit on the north-east part of Alder's island and put up a little shack overnight – well, you can see what would happen. Alder would . . .'

Mason broke off abruptly as a red spotlight suddenly blazed into brilliance ahead. A motor-cycle officer motioned Mason to one side, said, 'Get in line behind those other cars. Move up slowly.'

31

There were a dozen cars ahead, and several officers were examining credentials, asking questions.

Mason exchanged glances with Della Street, then eased the car forward as one of the officers said, 'May I see your driving licence and the car registration, please?'

Mason showed him the documents.

'You've been down here . . . Oh, oh, you're Perry Mason, the lawyer.'

'That's right.'

The officer smiled and said, 'Pardon me for stopping you, Mr Mason. It's okay, go ahead. We're looking for some gem thieves. You can detour right around those other cars and around the end of the road block. Sorry I bothered you . . . However, as a matter of routine, I'd better check the person with you because it was a woman who . . .'

'Miss Della Street, Mr Mason's secretary,' Della Street said, handing the officer her driving licence.

He checked the driving licence, glanced at her, handed the licence back, and said, 'Sorry, but we've been instructed to make a check. Down here on business, Mr Mason?'

'Just looking up some witnesses,' Mason said, non-committally.

Another car, which had been coming up fast, screamed to a stop as the red light stabbed through the windshield and the motor-cycle officer motioned the car to the side of the road.

'Okay,' Mason said, 'be seeing you,' and eased on around the road block.

Back on the main road, Mason once more urged the car into speed.

'Chief,' Della Street said, suddenly serious, 'do you suppose that girl did steal any jewels?'

'I don't think so.'

'But you don't know?'

'I looked her over pretty thoroughly, Della. She had a bottle in her right hand, a bottle containing a note which had apparently been thrown overboard from the *Thayerbelle*, George Alder's yacht, by a woman who was afraid she was going to be murdered and who was subsequently found dead.'

'Chief!' Della Street exclaimed.

'And,' Mason went on. 'I looked her over pretty carefully to make certain there wasn't anything concealed.'

'Did you look in the tops of her stockings?'

'Not in the *tops* of her stockings,' Mason said, 'but when she climbed over the front of the canoe, I saw a pair of very symmetrical legs with no ugly bulges such as would have been made by fifty thousand dollars' worth of jewellery. A wet dinner gown leaves but very, very little to the imagination.'

'Did you get her name?'

'Dorothy Fenner was the name she gave. She's supposed to be related to Corrine, the half sister who's been missing for several months.'

'Looks?'

'Lots.'

'Figure?'

'Swell.'

Della Street said, 'Well, boys will be boys.'

Mason said, 'Now that we're past the road block I'll let you read something.'

He took from his pocket the copy of the letter which Dorothy Fenner had made, and handed it to Della Street.

'What's this?'

'A copy of the letter that was in the bottle. The girl is a good typist. I held the flashlight and read the original letter to her. She balanced a portable typewriter on her knees and made a copy.'

Della Street unfolded the pages, switched on the map light on the dashboard, and read with increasing interest. When she had finished, she said, 'Good heavens, Chief, doesn't that letter give us a stranglehold on George S. Alder?'

'Or else it gives George S. Alder a stranglehold on me.'

'You mean that the whole thing was a plant?'

'That,' Mason said, 'is what's worrying the hell out of me. Alder knows I'm representing that syndicate. He *could* have made a pretty shrewd guess that I was going to drop by and look his island over, and after all I didn't see where this swimming girl came from. The first thing I knew she was sliding along through the water, then she reached the island, walked out to stand outlined against the light of that illuminated NO TRESPASSING sign, and started drying herself with a towel. One can't imagine anything better calculated to arrest the attention of a prowling canoeist.'

'And you with your binoculars!' Della Street said, laughingly.

'Me with my binoculars and my damn curiosity, leading with my chin. The whole thing was perfectly timed. After her discovery, the girl had just enough head start to reach the water in front of my canoe before they turned the dog loose. And the dog was right at her heels. Naturally I pushed the dog away and invited the girl to get in. She was good-looking, casually flippant – she didn't seem like a thief – and you have to admit the approach was unusual.'

'But,' Della Street said, 'you took precautions, you . . .'

'I *thought* I was taking precautions,' Mason said. 'She was wearing a strapless dinner gown without a darn thing underneath it except a pair of stockings. She made a point of displaying this bottle quite prominently – and then, of course, when I read what was in the bottle, I realised it was right down my alley. You couldn't have asked for a better trap.'

'Better bait, you mean.'

'It's the same thing.'

They drove in silence for a while, then Della Street said, 'And then George Alder announces she took fifty thousand dollars' worth of jewels and had a male accomplice waiting in a boat. Just where does that leave you, Chief?'

'Right behind the eight ball. If I'd done the obvious thing, told this girl who I was, persuaded her to let me take the letter – well, that would have left me *really* in a spot.'

'But, as it is, she doesn't know who you are,' Della Street pointed out.

'If it's a trap she does,' Mason said. 'In that case she knew before she ever swam ashore and started drying herself with a bath towel, which she conveniently left for the police to find – and I suppose there's a laundry mark on that bath towel which will enable the police to trace her.'

'Oh, oh.' Della Street said.

'Exactly,' Mason commented.

Della Street folded the copy of the letter, handed it back to Perry Mason.

'This letter is dynamite,' she said.

'It is, if it's true.'

'It looks to me as though you've really got him on the defensive,' Della Street said.

Mason said, 'Just who has whom on the defensive is one of those things that events will have to determine.'

She glanced up at him with eyes that were filled with confidence.

'You have a way of determining events,' she pointed out.

CHAPTER THREE

At nine-five Monday morning when Mason entered his office, Della Street, her finger on her lips, looked up from the phone in Mason's private office, said into the mouthpiece, 'Yes, Mrs Brawley, yes, indeed. Could you hold the phone just a moment ? Someone is calling on the other phone.'

Della Street cupped her hand over the mouthpiece of the telephone, said rapidly to Perry Mason, 'Mrs Brawley, the matron at the jail in Las Alisas, has a prisoner there, a Dorothy Fenner, held on suspicion of a jewel robbery, who wants to consult an attorney, and wants you.'

'Oh, oh,' Mason said. 'It's a trap then. She knew who I was all along.'

'Perhaps she didn't, Della Street said, her hand still over the mouthpiece. 'Do you want me to send Jackson down there and let him talk with her ? That way you can find out whether it's just a coincidence or . . .'

Mason grinned. 'Thanks for the life-saver, Della. That's what we'll do.'

Della Street took her hand from the mouthpiece, said, 'Well, I'm not in a position to speak for Mr Mason, Mrs Brawley, but I'll tell you what we'll do. We'll have Mr Jackson, Mr Mason's clerk, come down and interview Miss Fenner. You say she's in for a jewel robbery . . . Yes . . . Oh, within half an hour or so. He should be on his way within thirty minutes . . . Yes . . . All right, thank you. Good-bye.'

Della Street hung up and cocked a quizzical eyebrow at her employer.

Mason said glumly, 'George S. Alder is now beginning to turn the screw in the vice. So this girl was really bait for a trap after all.'

'Is she really beautiful, Chief ?'

Mason nodded.

'Well,' Della Street said, 'that's one consolation. Her beauty will be utterly wasted on Carl Jackson. Jackson will see only the legal principles involved, and for the rest of it will regard her owlishly through those thick-lensed spectacles of his, blinking his eyes as though trying to chop the situation up into small pieces so he can more readily feed them into his mental digestive apparatus.'

Mason laughed. 'Good description, Della. I've never noticed it before but he does seem to be afraid to trust himself to look at a girl all at once.'

'A great believer in precedent,' Della Street said. 'I think if he were ever confronted with a really novel situation he'd faint. He runs to his law books, digs around like a mole and finally comes up with some case that's what he calls "on all fours" and was decided seventy-five or a hundred years ago.'

'At that you have to hand it to him,' Mason said. 'He always finds the case. He's an absolute terror to all of these young lawyers who take such things seriously. Turn Jackson loose in a law library and he'll come up with a whole handful of precedents. And the nice part of it is he finds the precedents that are in your favour. So many briefing clerks seem to have a knack of finding precedents that are dead against what your client wants to do.'

Della said mischievously, 'I always remember what you said about him when he got married.'

'What was that?' Mason asked, looking slightly alarmed.

'A conversation that I overheard you and Paul Drake having.'

'Tut, tut, you shouldn't listen in on such conversations, particularly at a time like that.'

'I know,' she admitted. 'That's why I was particularly careful to listen. I remember you told Paul Drake that he was marrying a widow because he was afraid of any situation for which he couldn't find a precedent.'

Mason laughed. 'I shouldn't have said it, but it's probably true. Get him in here, Della, and we'll start him working on Dorothy Fenner.'

'Will you tell him to use his judgment about . . .'

Mason shook his head and said, 'I'll tell him that we're going to represent her. I just want him to find out how she happened to get in touch with us. That's all.'

'But suppose it wasn't a trap? Suppose she doesn't know, and . . .'

'And would get some other attorney,' Perry Mason said. 'And then, midway through the trial, she'd happen to see my picture or catch a glimpse of me in court and blab out to this lawyer that I was the one they'd been referring to as the male accomplice. The lawyer would rush to the newspapers . . . You can imagine what a situation *that* would make! No, Della, we're in this and we're going all the way. If it's not a trap we'll give Alder a going over,

36

and if it *is* a trap, we'll smash our way out. Get Jackson in here.'

Della Street arose from her desk, walked rapidly through the door to the law library and on to Jackson's office beyond. A few moments later she came back with the blinking, beetle-browed Jackson a few steps behind her, peering owlishly through his thick-lensed glasses.

Mason said, 'Sit down, Jackson. There's a very interesting case down at the Las Alisas jail, a young woman whom we're going to represent. Her name's Dorothy Fenner. She's accused of having broken into the house of George S. Alder and stolen some fifty thousand dollars' worth of jewels.

'Now, we're going to represent her. I want that definitely understood. The question of a fee won't be particularly important but I do want to find out just how it happened that she asked me to represent her.'

Jackson blinked.

'Then,' Mason said, 'I want bail fixed for her, and when you get a judge to fix bail, I want you to make the claim that the fifty thousand dollars' worth of jewels is merely so much newspaper talk; that it's easy to say fifty thousand dollars in round figures, but that for the purposes of fixing bail we want to know exactly what jewellery was taken; otherwise we'll consider that the jewellery has only a nominal value and that bail should be fixed in a very nominal amount.'

Jackson nodded.

'Think you can do that? Mason asked. 'I – I mean, get a judge to inquire somewhat into the nature and extent of the property that was taken before fixing the amount of bail?'

'Well, of course I can try,' Jackson said, 'but as I remember the doctrine which was held in a case in the eighty-second California Reports ... Now, wait a minute, and I'll have it ... Don't prompt me, please.'

Jackson held up his right hand, started snapping the fingers. At the third snap, he said, 'Oh, yes, I have it. In re Williams, in the eighty-second California Reports, I think it's page one eighty-three, it was stated that the amount of bail should not depend upon the amount of money which may have been lost to one party or secured by another party by reason of the offence charged; but it was held that bail should depend rather upon the moral turpitude of the crime and the danger resulting to the public from the commission of the offence.'

37

Mason grinned. 'Just after I'd finished telling Della Street what a whiz you were at digging up precedents that were in favour of our clients rather than against them.'

'Well, of course,' Jackson went on judicially, 'a great deal, a very great deal, would depend upon the *character* of the young woman; and, of course, the circumstances under which the property was alleged to have been taken. For the purpose of setting bail, it will be necessary to assume that the charge is well-founded.'

Mason said, 'Just walk in there with your fighting clothes on and get in touch with whatever deputy district attorney is handling the thing and demand that he get hold of the complaining witness. Insist that we want to get a specific allegation as to what was taken and exactly when it was taken and the value of it. And, above all, find out whether this young woman got in touch with me because of my reputation, because someone told her to give me a ring, or because she thinks she knows me.'

'*Do* you know her?' Jackson asked, blinking inquiringly at Mason.

'How the hell do I know? Jackson, in my position would you know everyone who had served on a jury, everyone who had been a witness in a case?'

'No, sir, I don't think I would.'

'I don't think you would either,' Mason said, picking up some papers. 'Skip down to the Las Alisas jail and get hold of this Dorothy Fenner. Tell her not to worry. Get started as fast as you can. We want some action. File a habeas corpus if you have to.'

When Jackson had gone, Mason turned to Della Street. 'He does ask the damnedest questions.'

'Doesn't he? And at the most unexpected times. Then you look at that impassive countenance of his and those eyes blinking away at you as though you were some sort of a bug he was looking at through a microscope and you're darned if you know whether the guy is *really* smart, or just intelligent.'

Mason threw back his head and laughed.

'Get hold of Paul Drake for me, Della. Let's start some detectives working.'

Della Street dialled Paul Drake's unlisted number on the confidential line which Mason kept in his private office, detouring the outside switchboard, and in a moment said, 'Hello, Paul? This is Della . . . How busy are you? . . . Do you suppose you could run down to the office? . . . That's fine. Right away, eh?'

She raised inquiring eyebrows at Mason, caught his nod, said,

'That'll be fine, Paul. The Chief will be expecting you. I'll be waiting at the door.'

She hung up the telephone and moved over to the exit door to the corridor from Mason's private office.

'He's coming right down,' she said.

Paul Drake, head of the Drake Detective Agency, had offices down the corridor near the elevator, and it was only a matter of seconds until Della Street heard his steps in the corridor. As soon as a dark shadow formed on the ground glass of the exit door, Della Street jerked back the latch and opened the door.

'Service,' Drake said, grinning amiably at them as he shuffled over to the big overstuffed client's chair and draped himself in his favourite position with his knees propped over one rounded arm of the chair, the other rounded arm furnishing support for his back.

'What's the pitch ?' he drawled, elevating one knee and clasping his fingers around the shin-bone as he glanced from Mason to Della Street.

'You're a hell of a detective,' Mason told him. 'You always look as though you were about ready to fall apart.'

'I know,' Drake said. 'It's my disguise. Underneath this thin head of hair, back of these glassy eyes, is a ball-bearing brain racing away like mad.'

'Perhaps that's why it's so darned hard to get you started in a new direction,' Mason said. 'Your brain is just a huge gyroscope.'

'It makes for stability,' Drake told them, 'and enables me to hold great quantities of liquor.'

'Liquor doesn't affect it ?' Della Street asked.

'Just makes it go around faster,' Drake assured her. 'I'm charging somebody for this time. Did you bring me down here to ask questions about my brains ?'

'Heaven forbid,' Mason said. 'We want you to find out something about a nice murder case.'

'Murder cases are never nice,' Drake told him, 'particularly your murder cases.'

'This is a swell murder case,' Mason said. 'It involves a Miss Minerva Danby, evidently a curvaceous exponent of feminine pulchritude, who is supposed to have been drowned by slipping overboard from a yacht . . .'

'You mean the Alder case ?' Drake interrupted.

'You know about it ?'

'I remember about it,' Drake said. 'I remember because of the large amounts of whitewash that were spilled over everything in sight. The officials all seemed to vie with each other in grabbing Alder, shaking his hand and pouring white paint all over the boy.'

'Remember any of the facts?' Mason asked innocently, glancing surreptitiously at Della Street.

'Well,' Drake said, 'this George Alder is quite some pumpkins. He has a big yacht that's a miniature ocean liner, all fitted out with teakwood, mahogany, brass and polish, telephones all over the boat, a private bar, stewards and all that stuff. He owns a big place on an island . . . Hey, wait a minute, that must have been the Alder whose house was burglarised last night.'

'What about it?' Mason asked.

'Oh, just a piece in the paper. Some woman put on a dinner gown, mingled with guests, copped fifty thousand bucks in jewellery; and made her escape by water. A male accomplice was sitting out there playing it safe, sending the girl in to do the dirty work. When she ran out, he slipped in with the canoe and picked her up, then whisked her out of harm's way. At that, they almost caught them by breaking out some motorboats and getting an early start. Eventually, they traced her through a bath towel.'

Mason said, 'Well, I want to find out all about Alder; I want to find out about Minerva Danby's death, and if you want to let various and sundry people know that that death is being investigated, it's all right by me.'

'Newspapers?' Drake asked.

'Not *too* obvious,' Mason said, 'Perhaps a veiled reference to the fact that your agency is asking questions around Catalina Island, trying to determine additional facts about the mysterious death of a young woman who was reported to have been swept away by rough seas from the yacht of a multimillionaire . . . You know, that vague sort of stuff.'

'Papers don't go so much for that stuff,' Drake said, 'but I know a couple of columnists who would like to get a lead. That is, if it's on the up-and-up.'

'It's on the up-and-up. Go ahead and start your investigation. Find out anything you can.'

'Okay. Anything else?'

'Keep an ear to the ground on that jewel burglary. Try and find out *if* that's what it *really* was.'

'Gosh, Perry, you think there's any chance it could have been . . .'

'I don't know.' Mason told him. 'Get busy and find out. Ask

questions; put men to work; find out everything you can about Alder. I want a complete picture.'

'How many men do I put to work on it?' Drake asked.

'As many as you have to.'

'To get information by what time?'

'As soon as you can.'

Drake said, 'You're leaving yourself wide open, Perry. I have a lot of men I can draw on now. Business isn't any too good, and ...'

'Start 'em working,' Mason told him. 'Just don't have them falling all over each other, or getting in each other's way, but have them make inquiries, and really go to town.'

'And we don't have to make it hush-hush?'

'As far as I'm concerned,' Mason told him, 'you can hire a brass band.'

'Okay,' Drake said, 'that saves a lot of trouble. It means we won't have to waste time beating around the bush.'

'Another thing,' Mason said. 'I want you to look up the date Minerva Danby died. Then check back on the records at Los Merritos. You'll find that at that time there was a woman undergoing treatment at that institution. This woman couldn't give any definite account of herself. She was suffering from a sort of amnesia, and apparently had no relatives. —

'Look up Corrine Lansing. Get her age, build, colour of eyes, and all that. Find out what you can about her disappearance. She's a half sister to George Alder. Anyway, get all the dope and get it fast.'

'Okay, anything else, Perry?'

'I want a complete job on Alder. I want to know everything I can about him. If he has any weak points I want to find out about them. That is, any weak chinks in his armour.'

Drake slid down out of the chair. 'Okay, Perry, I'll get to work.'

Mason waited until he had gone, then turned to Della Street. 'Get hold of the surety company; tell them I'll want them to put up bail within a short time in that Dorothy Fenner case; tell them to make any inquiries they want about Dorothy Fenner, but that I'll stand behind any bail bond that's issued, and that I want them in a position to issue one fast when the time comes.'

Della Street turned to the telephone.

'You'd better talk with the manager personally,' Mason said. 'Tell him that I'll appreciate some prompt action on this.'

'I'll tell him it's a *personal* favour,' she said.

'No cracks,' Mason warned.

'That wasn't a crack, it was a break.' Della Street started dialling the number.

CHAPTER FOUR

Jackson cleared his throat, deposited his briefcase on the table, started methodically taking out papers.

'Did you get the bail fixed?' Mason asked.

Jackson said, 'Perhaps I'd better take it up in chronological order and tell you exactly what happened. I . . .'

'Did you get the bail fixed?'

'Not yet. The matter has been taken under advisement by Judge Lankershim.'

'Taking a matter of bail under advisement?' Mason asked incredulously.

'Well, the Judge intimated that he would consider a bail of $25,000 in case he was called upon for an immediate decision. He wished to confer with the district attorney's office and intimated that he would make a sharp reduction in the amount of bail in the event he felt that it would be safe to do so. He says he will take the matter up at four o'clock this afternoon, immediately at the close of a late calendar he's calling.'

Mason glanced at his watch.

Jackson said, 'I went to the Las Alisas jail and discussed the matter with this young woman. She knows you only by reputation and has never even seen you. She wants to get the best attorney available but, as is quite usually the case with persons who demand the best, her financial resources are limited.

'However, in view of the fact that I had been definitely advised we would take the case I did not discuss the matter of emolument with here at any length, but merely made an attempt to ascertain her financial background.

'Apparently she has a small amount of money. She is an expert typist, stenographer, and secretary, and is employed at a fair salary. She has some eight or nine thousand dollars which is left from an insurance policy her mother took out in her favour. She is quite a yachting enthusiast and owns a small yacht which wouldn't sell for very much. She has sailed on several yachts, knows the yachting crowd, and apparently is rather popular with them. Her own yacht is a relatively small affair which she picked up at . . .'

'Never mind that,' Mason said. 'What about the case?'

'She insists that she did not steal any jewellery. She fails to account for the presence of the bath towel, bathing cap and a rubber sack at the scene of the crime. Apparently she is not able to furnish an alibi. She was aboard her yacht at the time of the burglary. She tells a very peculiar story about someone getting aboard her yacht during her absence and stealing something which belonged to her. She intimates, without making a direct accusation, that Mr Alder knows about this. She says further that when she can get in touch with some mysterious man, whose name she either can't or won't divulge, that she expects to be able to prove some rather serious charge against Mr Alder, but I cannot ascertain the exact nature of that charge. Strangely enough she says this mysterious man is a lawyer. She feels certain he would help her out but she either doesn't know his name or claims she doesn't. She has, of course, heard a lot about you and insists she needs the best lawyer available. She is personally acquainted with George S. Alder and seems to be very much afraid of him.

'I wish to state frankly that I am not favourably impressed with this young woman. She acts guilty to me. However, following instructions I told her you would represent her. She wants to talk with you personally. I am afraid I did not create an especially favourable impression, and I must confess that any personal lack of confidence was mutual. Her story is far from being straightforward.'

'Is she to be in court at four o'clock this afternoon?'

'Judge Lankershim said nothing about her being there. He asked that a representative of this office and of the district attorney's office gather with him to discuss the matter.'

'Who's handling the case for the DA?'

'Vincent Colton.'

Mason glanced at Della Street, 'What appearance does she make, Jackson? Good-looking?'

Jackson deliberated a moment, blinked reflectively, and said, 'I believe she is, Mr Mason,' as though the thought had just struck him.

'Think she'd make a good impression on a jury?'

Again Jackson digested that thought with slow, blinking appraisal.

'I believe she could.'

'And Vincent Colton wanted a continuance in the matter ?'

'He intimated there might be some clarification of the position of the district attorney by late this afternoon.'

'But you don't think this young woman had any direct lead to our office ? It was simply a matter of . . .'

'Of wanting the best.' She'd heard a great deal about you and – well, at least she was willing to make a stab at it. Of course her idea of a fee is probably in nowise commensurate with the work involved. I didn't discuss that phase of the matter.'

Mason glanced at his watch, said, 'Okay, I'll run along. I'll be seeing you folks later. Della, you might wait for a ring from me before you go home.'

She nodded.

'Thanks, Jackson,' Mason said.

'In such matters,' Jackson said, with stiff formality, 'I have at times a feeling of utter inadequacy. It is particularly embarrassing when one is thoroughly conversant with every phase of the law, to have a layman adopt a position of – well, frankly, Mr Mason, of doubt.'

'It certainly is,' Mason said. 'Okay, I'll take over now, Jackson. Just forget about it.'

Jackson's sigh of relief was plainly audible. 'Come to think of it, Mr Mason,' he said, 'now that you've mentioned the matter, she really is what you might call attractive. Sort of a blonde with a very good complexion and . . .'

'Good figure ?' Della asked mischievously.

'Oh, heavens, I wouldn't know about that,' Jackson said. 'In fact, it is with some effort I am recalling the colour of her eyes and hair, but the general impression, the over-all impression which would be made on a jury would, I should say, be favourable, distinctly so.'

Mason said, 'Well, I'll take over. Here's something you can start working on, Jackson. As I understand the law, any increase to property due to accretion and caused by the elements belongs to the landowner.'

'Yes, sir. There are dozens of decisions . . .'

'But when it's an accretion caused by a governmental activity such as building a breakwater or dredging a channel, the accretion becomes government property. In which event it might be subject to location by a citizen.'

Jackson made furrows in his forehead. 'Well, now, let's see. That's rather a fine distinction. I'm afraid, Mr Mason . . . No, by

George! Wait a minute ... You're right! The leading case is City of Los Angeles versus Anderson, in the 206th California. That case, I believe, dealt with land formed adjacent to a government breakwater. I can't be certain it would apply to some other governmental activity such as dredging. Yet the principle would seem to be the same.'

'Look it up,' Mason said. 'I want a leg to stand on. Make it as strong as you can.'

'Yes, sir, and am I to understand that you'll take over on this bail matter? It would be extremely annoying if ...'

'I'm taking over,' Mason said. 'You just concentrate on the problem of accretion due to governmental activity.'

Mason grabbed his hat, drove to the Las Alisas sheriff's office, secured a pass and telephoned the matron. 'I want to see Dorothy Fenner,' he said. 'This is Perry Mason.'

'Oh, Mr Jackson from your office was here this morning. He talked with her.'

'He did, did he?' Mason said. 'Well, I'll talk with her myself.'

'All right. I'll bring her down to the visitors' room. She ... she's been crying.'

'That's fine,' Mason said. 'I'll try and cheer her up a bit.'

'I think she's feeling rather depressed.'

'Okay,' Mason said, 'I'll meet you in the visitors' room.'

The lawyer went up in the elevator, presented his pass and waited until the matron brought a swollen-eyed Dorothy Fenner into the room, a room with a long table, through the middle of which ran a heavy screen dividing the room into two separate rooms.

The matron said, 'Come on over here, dearie. Here's Mr Mason. He wants to talk with you.'

Dorothy Fenner walked over to the screen as one in a daze, then suddenly jerked to startled attention. 'Why, you're ...'

'Perry Mason,' Mason interrupted. 'And very pleased to meet you, Miss Fenner.'

'Why, what I mean is that you're ...'

'Perry Mason,' the lawyer interrupted, significantly.

'Oh,' she said, and sat down as though her legs were buckling.

The matron smiled, patted her back reassuringly, said, 'How's everything, Mr Mason?'

'Fine,' Mason told her.

'Let me know when you're ready,' the matron said, and withdrew out of earshot.

Dorothy Fenner raised her head and surveyed Mason through the screen with incredulous eyes.

She looked back over her shoulder to make certain no one was within earshot and then said in a low voice, 'Why . . . why didn't you tell me?'

Mason said, 'Can't you appreciate my position? You were committing an illegal act.'

'What are you going to do now?'

'The first thing I'm going to do,' Mason said, 'is get you out on bail, but I want to know exactly what happened.'

She said, 'I guess I was a little fool, Mr Mason. I didn't do what you told me to. I had a bear by the tail, but I wasn't ready to go to George Alder. I thought I'd talk with Pete Cadiz about finding the bottle. I wanted time to think things over.'

'So what did you do?'

She said, 'I concealed that bottle where I thought it would never be found.'

'Where?'

'In the fresh-water tank on my yacht. I unscrewed the cleaning plug on the drinking water tank and put the bottle inside.'

'Then what?'

'Then I went ashore to take the inter-urban for town, feeling very satisfied with myself.'

'You have an automobile?'

'No. My one extravagance is the yacht. I love yachting. On the whole it costs me a lot less to keep this yacht than it would a car, and . . .'

'Okay,' Mason interrupted, 'what happened?'

She said, 'I stopped in at a little restaurant for breakfast yesterday morning, read the papers, and learned about what Alder was saying. That someone had broken into his house and taken fifty thousand dollars in gems and – well, suddenly I realised that he had me. He'd been smart enough not to say anything at all about losing the bottle with the letter in it, but simply claimed that I'd broken in in order to steal jewels. And, of course, like a little simp, not intending to get caught in any such mess, I had left myself wide open. And then I realised that you were my only hope because you – of course I didn't know who you were at the time – could swear I hadn't taken any jewels from the house.'

'So what did you do?' Mason asked.

'Well,' she said, 'at that late date I decided to follow your

46

advice. I went back to the yacht, deciding that I'd get this bottle with the letter and . . .'

'You'd put the letter back into the bottle?'

'Yes. Just the way I found it. Corked and all.'

'All right, what happened?'

'Well, when I went back to the yacht the bottle was gone. I was absolutely thunderstruck. I couldn't believe it possible. I searched and searched, and then I pumped every blessed bit of water out of that water tank and looked in it with the flashlight. That bottle simply had disappeared.'

Mason said, 'You're dealing with a shrewd individual, Dorothy. He knew who had the bottle. He simply waited until you had gone ashore, and then he went aboard and started searching the yacht. Evidently he's a pretty good yachtsman and as such figured out the places where something like that could be hidden. So now he has the bottle and the letter and has enough evidence against you so he can convict you of breaking into his house. Is that right?'

'I guess so, yes . . . I . . . I suppose I must have left fingerprints. Like a ninny I didn't wear gloves . . . oh, what a mess it is.'

Mason nodded.

'Well,' she said, 'there's one thing. You can back up my story and now we can tell the truth. Oh, I'm so relieved, so glad to see you, Mr Mason. I wondered how I was ever going to get in touch with the only man in the world who could show that I hadn't taken those jewels . . .'

'Take it easy,' Mason said. 'You can't handle it that way.'

'Why not?'

'Because if we tell that story now, it's going to look like an attempt to fabricate evidence so we can try and build up a case against Alder. Everyone will laugh at us for not thinking up a better lie than that.

'Furthermore, when I put myself in the position of being interested in the letter that was in that bottle, and then letting you take it and put it in the water where someone could come and steal it, and all we can show is a typewritten copy of what we *claim* the letter was . . . No, my dear, I'm afraid we can't do that.'

'Then what *can* we do?'

Mason grinned, and said, 'Ever hear the story about the American who went to the foreign country and got into trouble with one of the slick business men there?'

'No, what about it?'

Mason said, 'It's a legal classic. The business man sued the

47

American for a large sum of money which he claimed he had loaned the American with which to start a business venture. The American went to a lawyer, complained bitterly, and wanted to go on the stand and swear that it was a complete falsehood.

'The attorney carefully listened to the American's story, smiled benignly, and said he would fix things all up.

'Imagine the American's surprise when the case came up in the foreign court. The business man got on the stand and swore that he had loaned the American this sum of money and then called five witnesses; two of them swore that they had seen the money loaned to the American, and three of them testified that the American had told them about having borrowed the money from this foreign business man and hoped to be able to pay it back out of profits.'

'What happened?' she asked, interested.

'The American's lawyer didn't even cross-examine the witnesses, and the American almost had a fit,' Mason said. 'His lawyer explained to him that in this country it was rather easy to get witnesses to commit perjury for a reasonable consideration. The American saw ruination staring him in the face. Then it came his turn to put on his defence and his lawyer urbanely called seven witnesses, each of whom stated that he knew that the American had borrowed money from this business man, but that he had been present in the room when the American had paid it back, every cent of it.'

A wan smile twisted her lips. 'And what's the moral of that story, Mr Mason?'

'It isn't a moral, it's an "immoral",' Mason told her. 'It means that there are times when you have to fight the devil with fire.'

'So what do we do?'

'At the moment it's what we *don't* do. We don't go rushing into court and say anything about the bottle. We don't show the copy of the letter that we made. I do wish we'd had a camera so that we could have photographed that document. Then we'd have been in an entirely different position. But we didn't have, so there you are, or rather, *here* you are.'

'But, Mr Mason, don't you see what he's done? He's – why, if we let him get away with that, if he can put us in that position, I've lost my evidence, I can't ever say anything about it later on, and – and, good lord, I *did* break into his house and he could have me convicted of a felony and . . .'

'You leave it to me,' Mason said. 'I'm not too certain, but what

48

your friend, George S. Alder, may get something of a shock when he learns that I'm going to represent you. Keep a stiff upper lip, Dorothy, and you may be out of here by dinner-time.'

'By dinner-time, Mr Mason? Why, even if a judge made an order admitting me to bail, my financial resources are . . .'

Mason said, 'I have quite a bit at stake myself. If it hadn't been for . . . oh well, you see now how it was. I couldn't possibly have done anything there Saturday night without making it appear that we'd been engaged in some sort of a scheme, either to concoct or steal evidence, and either would have been bad for me.'

'Oh, if I'd only gone to Alder, the way you told me to. But I thought I knew more. If I'd only known who you were, I'd have taken your advice unquestioningly.'

'Well,' Mason said, 'we're in it now, and we'll see it through.'

'What are you going to do?'

Mason said, 'I'm going to use a little ingenuity for one thing, and perhaps a little bluff. The first thing you're going to do is to get out on bail. The next thing we're going to do is to sue George S. Alder, and serve notice that we want to take his deposition. And *then* we're going to have him worried.'

'But can you do all that?' she asked.

'We can try,' Mason said. 'Keep your chin up, Dorothy. I'll be seeing you later.'

Mason motioned to the matron the interview was over.

CHAPTER FIVE

Judge Lankershim listened patiently to the concluding arguments of a long-winded lawyer and said, 'The demurrer is overruled. Ten days to answer.'

He glanced at the clock, and said: 'That winds up the calendar. Now we have a matter which I have continued until this time. It involves the question of bail in the case of People versus Fenner.'

Vincent Colton said, 'We're ready to discuss the matter for the prosecution, Your Honour.'

Judge Lankershim said, 'Mr Jackson, of Mr Mason's office, was . . . Oh, I see Mr Mason is here himself. Are you ready to proceed, Mr Mason?'

'Yes, Your Honour.'

'Now, what seems to be the trouble?' Judge Lankershim asked. 'Apparently a young woman is charged with theft. As I gathered the situation from Mr Jackson, any attempt at escape on her part would be exceedingly unlikely. She has money in the bank, owns a yacht, and . . .'

'And the money in the bank could be drawn out overnight,' Colton snapped. 'The yacht is an old, small boat, of very questionable value. This young woman has no previous criminal record, so far as I know, but the fact remains that she *did* enter this dwelling house during the night-time, mingled with the guests at a dinner party, and stole some fifty thousand dollars' worth of jewellery. To permit her to go free on a nominal bail would simply enable her to put up the five or ten thousand dollars bail, sell the jewellery, and be forty thousand dollars to the good.'

'Nonsense,' Mason said.

'Just a minute, Mr Mason,' Judge Lankershim interposed. 'You'll have an opportunity to state your case. Go on, Mr Deputy District Attorney.'

'That about covers the situation,' Colton said. 'Our office feels that this is a case where bail should be at least as high as the property that was taken.'

'None of the property has been recovered by the police?'

'No, Your Honour.'

Judge Lankershim thought for a moment, then glanced over his glasses at Perry Mason. 'Well, Mr Mason, what's the situation from your viewpoint? I think I have most of your views. Mr Jackson made a rather complete presentation of the case when I was approached in chambers. Mr Colton said he wanted time to correlate some other evidence.'

Mason said, 'In the first place, I don't think fifty thousand dollars' worth of jewellery was taken. I don't think any jewellery was taken.'

'I see,' Colton said sarcastically. 'Mr Alder, a very reputable and established citizen, is going around hurling false charges at innocent persons. Is that your contention?'

'You might be surprised,' Mason said, 'to know that it is. I'd just like to have Mr Alder make a list of the articles of jewellery which he claims were taken.'

'I've told him to prepare such a list,' Colton said.

'And then submit it to you?'

'Yes.'

'Under oath?'

'That's not necessary. He'll give his testimony when he gets to court.'

'Where is he now?'

'In my office, making out the list.'

Mason said, 'How long do you suppose it's going to take him to make it out?'

'Well, there were quite a few items.'

'I'd just like to know some of the items,' Mason said. 'I'd like to have him definitely show where he gets this figure of fifty thousand dollars.'

'He'll show at the proper time.'

'The proper time is right now, if he's going to try to prevent this young woman from being admitted to a reasonable bail.'

Mason turned and addressed himself to the judge. 'Your Honour, here is a young woman of position and refinement, and I think if you could see her you would appreciate immediately that there certainly must be some misunderstanding. I haven't as yet talked with her enough to know about all the facts of the defence. I understand that the only evidence which connects her with the crime is a bath towel, which had her laundry mark on it, on the premises.

'Obviously, any person who would steal fifty thousand dollars' worth of jewellery could steal a bath towel. I also doubt very much if any such amount of jewellery was taken. I think that the victim made a hurried guess to the police officers and I venture to say that if Mr Colton would get his office on the phone right now he'd find that Mr Alder is not only having exceedingly great difficulty in preparing such a list, but that he can't even list *any* jewellery which has been taken.'

'Oh, that's absurd,' Colton said.

Mason said, 'What's the use of bothering with a lot of affidavits? We have the judge here on the bench, ready to hear the matter. If, as you say, Alder is in your office at the present time, why not have him take the elevator and come to court?'

'And if he says fifty thousand dollars' worth of jewellery was taken you'll agree to a fifty thousand dollar bail?' Colton asked.

Mason said, 'Put your man right on that witness-stand. Ask him the question under oath. Give me an opportunity to ask a question or two on cross-examination to clarify the situation. If he then says fifty thousand dollars' worth of jewellery was taken, I'll submit that the bail should be fifty thousand dollars. Let's also have it agreed that if he says ten thousand dollars' worth of

51

jewellery was taken the bail will be ten thousand, and, if he says one thousand dollars' worth of jewellery was taken, the bail will be one thousand dollars, and, if he says no jewellery was taken, the defendant can be released on her own recognisance.'

'If he says no jewellery whatever was taken,' Colton said grimly, 'I'll not only let the defendant be released on her own recognisance, I'll dismiss the case.'

'All right, bring him in,' Mason said.

'If I may use the phone, Your Honour.'

'Go ahead. Take the telephone in my chambers,' Judge Lankershim said.

The deputy district attorney went to the judge's chambers. Judge Lankershim glanced somewhat quizzically over his glasses at Perry Mason. 'I see you took the matter over personally, Mr Mason.'

Mason nodded.

'Your Mr Jackson made a very able presentation of the law,' Judge Lankershim said.

'I'm glad he did, Your Honour. I'm going to try and make an equally able presentation of the facts.'

Judge Lankershim's eyes twinkled.

Vincent Colton returned to the court-room and said, 'Mr Alder will be right up.'

'Did you ask him if he had that list?' Mason asked.

Colton said with dignity, 'I told him to bring the list, and he could read it into evidence.'

Mason said, 'I want the court reporter to report this testimony.'

'It will be reported,' the court reporter said.

'And I want a transcript.'

'I'll take a copy,' Colton snapped.

They waited a few moments, and then the door opened and a spare, tight-lipped man in a double-breasted grey business suit walked into the court-room with an air of quiet, competent authority.

'George S. Alder,' Colton announced. 'Just come forward and be sworn, and take the stand, Mr Alder.'

Alder, his keen grey eyes from underneath level brows glancing around the court-room, then coming to rest somewhat curiously on Perry Mason, held up his right hand and was sworn.

'Just sit down there on the witness-stand,' Colton said. 'You have a list of the jewellery that was taken?'

'I have a very partial list. I find that it's a little difficult to trust

52

to my memory in these matters. I really would prefer to return home and take a complete inventory in order to make certain.'

'Well, can you tell the Court generally just about the value of the jewellery that was taken ?'

'I said approximately fifty thousand dollars, and I see no reason to change that figure,' Alder said, glancing quickly at Perry Mason, then back at Colton.

'You're *quite* certain that fifty thousand dollars' worth of jewellery was taken ?'

'Well,' Alder said, 'I, of course, am making an estimate – I haven't as yet made a complete inventory, and then, of course, it's a question whether you mean wholesale or retail price. But I would say that approximately fifty thousand dollars in jewellery had been taken.'

'I think that's all,' Colton said triumphantly.

'Just a couple of questions on cross-examination,' Mason said.

'Very well. Go ahead, Mr Mason,' Judge Lankershim said. 'This seems to be a routine matter and we're making quite a fuss about it. Let's try and get the matter disposed of. It seems to me that fifty thousand dollars bail is rather high, but if that amount was taken – and, of course, that's the stipulation which counsel entered into.'

'Quite right,' Mason said, 'I'm willing to be bound by my bargain, but I do want to ask a couple of questions.'

'Go ahead,' Judge Lankershim said, glancing at the clock.

'This jewellery insured ?' Mason asked casually.

'What does that have to do with it ?' Colton asked.

'Simply this,' Mason said, 'that if the jewellery *is* insured there will then be an inventory, together with values, attached to the insurance policy, and *this* might refresh Mr Alder's recollection.'

'Oh, I see. No objection.'

Alder said, 'Most of my jewellery is insured, yes.'

'Don't you carry a general all-purpose insurance policy with complete coverage on everything ?'

'Come to think of it, I believe I do, but the jewellery under that policy is ten per cent of the amount of the policy, I think.'

'And what's the amount of the policy ?'

'A hundred thousand dollars.'

'All right, there's ten thousand dollars' worth of jewellery. Then you have another insurance policy specifically on your jewellery ?'

'Yes, sir, I do.'

'In which the items are listed?'

'Well, some of them are listed.'

'All right,' Mason said, 'now, tell me one item of jewellery, just *one* item, mind you, that's covered in that specific insurance policy and which was taken from your house in this burglary.'

'I . . . I told you I'd have to make an inventory.'

'Just *one* item,' Mason said, holding up his index finger so that it emphasised the figure 'one'. 'Just one item of jewellery covered in that insurance policy.'

'I don't think I can do it, off-hand.'

'All right,' Mason said, 'now, tell me one item of jewellery that was taken that is *not* covered in that insurance policy.'

'Well, for one thing, there's a wrist-watch.'

'What make?'

'A rather expensive Swiss wrist-watch.'

'How do you know it was taken?'

'I haven't seen it – it seems to be missing.'

'All right,' Mason said. 'Now that wrist-watch would be covered in your other insurance policy, wouldn't it? The ten per cent of your all-purpose coverage.'

'I believe it would, yes.'

'So,' Mason said, 'you're going to make a claim to the insurance company for this wrist-watch in the event the police don't recover it. Is that right?'

'Well, I suppose so. I'm a busy man. I hadn't thought . . .'

'Yes or no,' Mason said. '*Are* you going to make a claim to the insurance company?'

'What does that have to do with it?' Colton asked.

'Just this!' Mason said. 'In the event that wrist-watch was *not* taken and this man makes a claim to an insurance company, he's going to be guilty of perjury and of obtaining money under false pretences, and I think he knows it. So he's not going to make any false statements in connection with a claim on an insurance policy. Now, then, Mr Alder, you're on oath. I want you to tell us one particular item of jewellery that was taken. Just one, any one.'

'Well, I saw this person, that is she had been discovered trying to steal things from my desk, and I . . . I went in there and opened the locked compartment where I keep jewels, and . . . well, I took a look at the jewel-box and estimated that a very large amount of jewellery had been taken.'

'Where did you get this jewellery?'

'Most of it came to me from my mother, after my father died.'

That is, it was part of father's estate. It was mother's jewellery.'

'And some of your own?'

'Wrist-watch, cuff-links, a diamond pin, a ruby ring . . .'

'Well, then,' Mason said, 'we shouldn't have any trouble, so let's list these things. Now, the diamond pin is gone, the ruby ring is gone, the . . .'

'I didn't say they were gone.'

'They're covered in the insurance policy?'

'I believe so, yes.'

'Well, are they gone, or aren't they?'

'I don't know. I tell you I didn't make a detailed inventory. I took a look at the contents of the jewel-box and estimated that about fifty thousand dollars' worth of jewellery had been taken.'

'Fifty thousand dollars,' Mason said, 'is quite a lot of jewellery.'

'Yes, sir.'

Alder moistened his lips, glanced somewhat appealingly towards the deputy district attorney.

'How much jewellery was in that box?'

'Quite a lot.'

'Insured?'

'Yes, sir.'

'How much was it insured for?'

'Fifty thousand dollars.'

'That was the value of it?'

'Yes, sir.'

'Then all of it must have been taken if fifty thousand dollars' worth of jewellery is missing.'

'Well, it wasn't all gone. I . . . I tell you I didn't take an inventory.'

'Why not?' Mason asked. 'Wasn't it good business for you to take an inventory?'

'Surely,' Judge Lankershim interrupted, 'you must have made some survey in order to find out what was missing, Mr. Alder.'

'Well, I didn't go through everything that was there, I was excited and . . . well, that was it, I was excited.'

'You're not excited now, are you?' Mason asked.

'No.'

'All right, tell us what was missing.'

'I haven't the jewel-box here.'

'Were you excited this morning before you went to the district attorney's office?'

'Of course there was the shock of having someone I'd trusted burglarise my house.'

'How much of a shock?'

'Quite a shock.'

'So much so that you couldn't concentrate on making a list of jewellery?'

'Well, I was excited, yes.'

'So, when you told the district attorney fifty thousand dollars in jewellery was taken, you were excited?'

'I don't see what that has to do with it.'

'You were so excited that you couldn't make an inventory of what jewellery was missing. Isn't that right?'

'Well, you might put it that way.'

'*I'm* not putting it that way,' Mason said, '*you* are. I'm simply trying to summarise your testimony. Now, isn't it quite possible that, when you said fifty thousand dollars, you had in mind the figure of the insurance policy, and . . .'

'I guess perhaps that's right, perhaps I could have.'

'Right now, at the present moment, you wouldn't swear that even ten thousand dollars' worth of jewellery was taken, would you?'

'Look here,' Alder said angrily, 'this young woman broke into my house; she was at my desk; my jewel-case was open. Someone opened the door and surprised her. One of the guests started to ask her what she was doing there, and the woman grabbed this bottle, and dashed for the window, and . . .'

Alder stopped abruptly.

'What bottle?' Mason asked.

'The bottle with the jewellery in it,' Alder said angrily.

'You keep your jewellery in a bottle?'

'I don't know. No, of course not, but it looked to some of the witnesses who saw her jump out of the window as though she had put the jewellery in a bottle or something. She had her escape all planned, and I suppose she didn't want to lose the jewellery in swimming. I don't know. All I know is some of the guests said a bottle.'

'*You* didn't see her?'

'Not close. I saw her running after she'd jumped through the window. I turned the dog loose. If he'd caught her, we'd have found how much of my property she had. She and that contemptible accomplice of hers!'

'No need to get worked up about it,' Mason said. 'We're simply

56

trying to get the matter straight. As far as you yourself are concerned, you don't *know* that even as much as two thousand dollars' worth of jewellery was taken, do you?'

'Well, I think . . .'

'You don't even *know* that one thousand dollars' worth of jewellery was taken.'

'I don't *know* anything was taken,' Alder said angrily. 'I took a look at that open jewel-box and it looked to me as though a great deal of stuff was missing.'

'But when you said fifty thousand dollars, you were thinking of the fact that the jewellery was insured for fifty thousand dollars. You were excited, and so you said fifty thousand dollars' worth of jewellery had been taken. Is that it?'

'Well, that might be an explanation.'

'You haven't made any claim on the insurance company?'

'No, sir.'

'And, as a matter of fact,' Mason said, pointing his finger at Alder, 'you don't intend to make any claim on the insurance company, do you?'

'I don't see where that has anything to do with it, and I don't think I have to sit here and be browbeaten about the matter,' Alder said.

Mason turned to Judge Lankershim. 'There you are, Your Honour. I'm willing to be bound by the stipulation. If he had said fifty thousand dollars had been taken, I'd have had the Court make fifty thousand dollars bail. As it is, he can't say that anything was taken. In which event, the district attorney agreed he would permit my client to be released on her own recognisance, and would dismiss the case, and . . .'

'Not so fast, not so fast,' Colton interposed. 'It's a far cry from browbeating and confusing this witness to . . .'

'I don't like that word browbeating,' Mason said. 'This man's a business man. He knows his rights. I'm simply asking him to make a direct, positive, unequivocal statement to this Court. He's afraid to do it. He's afraid to list any one particular item of jewellery and swear that this woman stole that item of jewellery, because he knows he can't prove it. It's one thing to tell newspaper reporters and the police that he's lost fifty thousand dollars' worth of jewellery, and it's another thing to prove it.'

'But why on earth would a man want to claim he'd lost fifty thousand dollars' worth of jewellery if he hadn't?' Judge Lankershim asked in perplexity. 'We have here no question of a publicity seeking individual who wants to see his name in the papers.'

'Because,' Mason said, 'for reasons of his own, he wanted the defendant apprehended.'

'Are you aware, Mr Mason, that that is a most serious charge?'

'I'm aware it's a most serious charge,' Mason said, 'and I'm so greatly aware of it that I can advise this Court and Mr Alder that the defendant, Dorothy Fenner, is going to bring suit against him for defamation of character, and then I'm going to take his deposition and when I get him on the witness-stand I'm going to defy him to produce *any* evidence of *any* single article of jewellery that was taken. Furthermore, I'm going to insist that representatives of the insurance company go to his house and make an inventory of the jewellery that's left, and check it against the items mentioned in the insurance policy.'

Mason ceased speaking, and there was a tense, dramatic silence.

That silence was broken at length by Colton, who said, 'It sounds to me as though Mr Mason is trying to intimidate the witness.'

'Well, listen again,' Mason said, 'and you'll find that I'm simply trying to protect my client against imposition.'

'This whole business is absurd,' Alder said. 'I was excited Saturday night, and I was confused yesterday morning. I didn't realise any lawyer was going to browbeat me . . .'

'You've used that word several times,' Judge Lankershim interrupted. 'This Court isn't going to let anyone browbeat you, Mr Alder, but the Court will ask you a question. Would you be willing for a representative of the Court to go to your house with you and check the contents of your jewellery chest against the inventory of the jewellery used for insurance purposes?'

'When?'

'Now.'

'It wouldn't be convenient now. I have other engagements.'

'All right then, you fix a time.'

There was an interval of silence, then Alder said, 'I'll go home and make that inventory myself. I'm a reputable citizen. There's no need to have all this fanfare. You'd think I was the thief – I already seem to be the defendant.'

Judge Lankershim pursed his lips.

Again there was a silence.

'Oh, well.' Judge Lankershim said. 'I'll admit the defendant to twenty-five hundred dollars bail.'

Mason picked up his briefcase and turned towards the door as Judge Lankershim left the bench.

'Say, what's the idea?' Colton asked Mason, his manner curious. 'Do you know anything about this burglary that I don't know?'

'Ask Alder,' Mason said.

Colton laughed grimly. 'Don't think I'm not going to do that very thing,' he said.

Alder left the witness-stand, seemingly trying to avoid both Mason and Colton.

Colton suddenly swung towards him. 'Don't leave, Mr Alder,' he said. 'I want you to go back to my office with me. I want to talk to you.'

'I have some other matters,' Alder said crisply, 'some appointments.'

'I don't think they are as important as this matter,' Colton told him. 'You'd better get this straightened out while we have the chance.'

Mason said to the clerk of the court, 'I'f you'll make me a certified copy of the judge's order, Mr Clerk, I'll see about getting my client released on bail.'

Colton nodded to Alder. 'This way, Mr Alder,' he said.

CHAPTER SIX

Perry Mason smiled at the matron, said to Dorothy Fenner, 'All right, Dorothy, get your things ready. You're going home.'

'What do you mean?' she asked, startled.

'You're getting out of here,' Mason told her. 'Judge Lankershim admitted you to twenty-five hundred dollars bail, and a surety company has put up the money.'

'But . . . but doesn't the surety company demand money from me as collateral security, or something?'

'Oh, I have an arrangement with them,' Mason said airily. 'You can get your things together and go on home. Where do you live, incidentally? I may be able to drive you home.'

'At the Monadnock Hotel Apartments.'

Mason said, 'I'm going to be busy. We stole a march on the

59

newspapers. No one expected any fireworks. We walked into court, and gave Alder a very bad ten minutes.'

'Did he say anything about the . . .'

Mason glanced significantly in the direction of the matron, and said. 'He started to let the cat out of the bag, and then tried to catch himself in time.'

The matron said with a laugh, 'Don't mind me, Mr Mason. I have one-way ears . . . Perhaps I'd better withdraw for a while. You have the bail bond and the order for release ?'

Mason handed her the papers.

'Okay,' she said, 'I'll be back here when you're ready to go. Now, if you'll excuse me a moment, I have another matter to attend to.'

She stepped out of the office.

Dorothy Fenner said in a quick, anxious voice. 'Wasn't *anything* said about the paper ?'

'Certainly not,' Mason said. 'He got excited and said something about a bottle, then he hastily tried to claim that you had a bottle to carry the jewels in.'

'All fifty thousand dollars' worth of them, I suppose,' she said bitterly.

'Well,' Mason grinned, 'that amount got whittled materially. It hadn't occurred to him that the insurance company might be interested in this. And then I dropped a bombshell by stating that we were going to sue him for defamation of character. I wouldn't be surprised if you heard from Mr Alder and found that he wanted to patch things up.'

'And what do I tell him ?'

Mason said, 'You tell him precisely this: "See my lawyer." That's all. Can you remember to tell him that ?'

'Yes.'

'And newspapermen may be calling on you,' Mason went on. 'I want you to tell them that you are not in a position to make any statement. Can you remember to do that ? Can I trust you ?'

'But, Mr Mason, what are we going to do now ? How are we ever going to get that paper that was in the bottle brought into evidence ? It seems to me now that we're – well, we're doing all this fighting just to get back to where we started.'

'That,' Mason told her, 'is what comes of not doing what I told you to do at the start. However, don't worry too much about the evidence now. Alder is on the defensive, and I don't think he likes being on the defensive. Now, let's get started.'

'Where are *you* going to be?' she asked. 'Can I get in touch with you – later on tonight if anything should develop?'

Mason said, 'If anything really important should turn up, ring up the Drake Detective Agency; that's a detective agency that has offices in the same building as mine and on the same floor. They're just to the right of the elevator as you leave the elevator. You ask for Paul Drake, and he'll know how to get a message to me, but don't call unless it's something very important, and don't let anyone stampede you into talking. They may try all sorts of tricks, but don't let them get away with it.'

She took his hand in both hers. 'Mr Mason,' she said, 'you . . . I can't . . .' Her voice choked up and tears were in her eyes.

'That's all right,' Mason told her. 'You just sit tight and carry on as though nothing had happened.'

She blinked back the tears. 'But, Mr Mason . . . somehow . . . that paper . . .'

'You leave all that to me,' Mason said.

'But I don't see how you can . . . unless I make a statement now . . .'

'You keep absolutely quiet,' Mason warned. 'Say nothing to anyone. Now we'll get the matron, have you released, and I'll drop you at your apartment house after we get to the city.'

CHAPTER SEVEN

Mason found Della Street waiting in the private office.

'Well,' she asked, 'what happened?'

Mason chuckled. 'Alder had to make *some* explanation to his guests. He said the unknown thief had broken into his house and stolen fifty thousand dollars' worth of gems. At the time he didn't realise that Dorothy Fenner had left a bath towel, bathing cap, and a rubber bag on his property near the illuminated sign, so he embellished the burglary with a lot of lurid details.

'Then, very much to his consternation, the police ran down the clue of the laundry mark on the towel and apprehended Dorothy.

'Naturally, Alder is a little flabbergasted. Then when I pointed out to him that all of his jewellery was insured, and the insurance company would expect him to make a claim of loss – and he knew damned well that the insurance company would be suspicious of the whole set-up – well, he began to lose his ardour very rapidly.'

Della Street said, 'You have a visitor waiting in the reception-room, Chief. He said he'd wait until I closed up the office no matter what time it was.'

'Who ?' Mason asked.

'Mr. Dorley H. Alder.'

Mason gave a low whistle.

'He told me he simply had to see you tonight.'

Mason, narrowing his eyes in thought, gave the matter careful consideration, then said, 'Try and fix the time when he came, Della. I want to find whether it was before or after George Alder began to realise he had a bear by the tail.'

'It must have been before. He's been waiting since, oh, I'd say since quarter past four.'

'Describe him, Della.'

'As far as looks are concerned, that's a cinch, but on his charac-yer it isn't so easy. He's in the middle sixties, well-dressed. well-preserved, shaggy-eyebrowed, and grey-haired. But there's something about the man which hits you with – well, not an impact, exactly. It catches you on your blind side. It's not exactly a benevolence. It's a quiet power – something in his manner and in the tone of his voice.'

'Let's take a look at him,' Mason said. 'He sounds interesting.'

'Definitely,' Della Street said. 'The man's interesting, but he's nobody's fool and I'll bet that this is the first time he's waited any length of time in anyone's reception-room.'

'Okay,' Mason said. 'Bring him in.'

The lawyer seated himself at his desk, pulled some letters towards him which Della Street had placed on his desk for signature, and said, 'I'll be signing mail when he comes in. It's the conventional thing to do, you know – appear busy.'

'You just keep right on signing them,' Della Street said, laughing. 'I want them to get in the mail tonight. I'll bring him in.'

Mason was signing the last of the letters when Della Street opened the door and said, 'Right in here, Mr Alder.'

Mason blotted the signature, dropped the pen back into its holder, and looked up to meet steady grey eyes which were surmounted by shaggy eyebrows.

'Mr Alder,' Mason said, arising and extending his hand.

Alder shook hands without actually smiling. His eyes softened into a twinkle for a moment, then were once more keen, hard and probing.

He was a thick, powerful man, and in repose his face had deeply etched lines which, together with the keen scrutiny of his eyes, gave an impression of calmness, and of poised power.

Dorley Alder seated himself comfortably in the big over-stuffed client's chair and seemed to fill it completely.

That big leather chair was one of Mason's most subtle psycho-logical weapons. The cushions were deep and soft. Clients who sat in it were inclined to relax physically and, in so doing, get off their guard, or, in more urgent matters, they would come forward to the extreme edge of the chair as though fearing to let themselves go.

Mason had worked out a system of card indexing clients based upon the manner in which they occupied this chair. Some tried to hide from the realities of the world in its protecting depths; others squirmed uneasily; but there were a few people who could sit there comfortably and fill the chair. Dorley Alder was one of these.

'I gather you wanted to see me about a matter of considerable importance,' Mason said.

'Mr Mason, are you familiar with our company – the Alder Associates, Incorporated?'

'I've heard something about it,' Mason said dryly.

'Do you know generally about the set-up?'

'Did you,' Mason countered, 'wish to consult me about that?'

'Not entirely,' Dorley Alder said, 'but I don't want to waste time telling you things you already know.'

'You might assume that I know nothing,' Mason said.

The frosty grey eyes hardened.

'That would be an insult to your intelligence and to mine, Mr Mason. You are representing a syndicate which holds a rather considerable acreage adjoining some of our holdings.'

Mason said nothing.

'And,' Dorley H. Alder went on, 'we happen to know the syndicate has been very anxious to sign an oil lease, but the drilling company will not go ahead with development work unless it can also control our acreage. Not only have we refused to consolidate our holdings with yours for the purposes of the lease, but, frankly, we were quite definitely manipulating things so as to force your clients to sell out their holdings for a fraction of their value. A little financial squeeze here, a little political pressure there. Under those circumstances, Mr Mason, to think that you would be *entirely* ignorant of the nature of our little corporation would be a reflection on your own abilities as an attorney, and my perspicacity as an opponent.'

'Go right ahead,' Mason said, grinning, 'it's your party. Start serving the refreshments whenever you get ready.'

A twinkle of humour softened Dorley Alder's eyes. There was something almost hypnotic about the calm cadences of his voice. 'I will assume that you *have* made such a survey, Mr Mason, that you have probed for points of weakness, and that you may perhaps have found some. As you are probably aware, the actual control of the corporation is in the hands of my nephew, George S. Alder.

'George is relatively a young man, Mr Mason. I am in the middle sixties. I am taking it for granted that you are familiar with the terms of the trust under which my brother left stock in the corporation.'

'That trust covers all the stock ?' Mason asked.

'All of it,' Dorley said.

'Very well,' Mason told him. 'Go ahead.'

'Corrine Lansing, George's half sister, had, of course, an equal interest.'

Mason merely nodded.

'She disappeared.'

Again Mason nodded.

'Under the circumstances,' Dorley Alder said, 'while there are some temporary expedients which we can resort to, we are advised that not until seven years have elapsed can we legally prove that she is dead.'

'No comment,' Mason said, smiling. 'I have enough trouble advising my own clients without checking another lawyer's opinions.'

'Of course,' Alder went on, 'that is true in case we have merely an unexplained disappearance. If we can find circumstantial evidence to indicate an actual death, that would be another matter.'

'I'm quite certain you didn't want to consult me about that,' Mason said.

Dorley said, 'I'm merely outlining a situation.'

'Go on with the outline.'

'In the event Corrine should still be alive, the situation in regard to the control of the company might change very drastically. At the present time under the trust, I am merely a minority stock-holder so far as votes are concerned. If Corrine were alive, I have reason to believe she would, perhaps, see things my way.'

'You had something specific in mind ?' Mason asked.

Dorley Alder said, 'Mr Mason, you and I are business men. Why not speak frankly ?'

'You're doing the talking, I'm listening frankly.'

Dorley Alder smiled, said, 'This little window dressing, Mr Mason, this story about the stolen gems. That's all right for the public, but for you and me the situation is different.'

'How different ?'

'I have reason to believe that Dorothy Fenner entered that house. I think she entered it for the purpose of getting a letter. I am very much interested in that letter.'

'How interested ?'

'*Quite* interested.'

'And precisely what do you know about the letter ?' Mason asked.

'I know that a letter was found by a beachcomber. I know that letter had been written on the stationery of the *Thayerbelle*, which is George's yacht. I understand that it was written by Minerva Danby, a woman who was washed overboard and drowned during a sudden, very severe storm.'

'And what else do you want to know ?' Mason asked.

'I would like to know very, very much what that letter con-tained.'

Mason studied the man thoughtfully. 'Do you want to know the contents of the letter, or merely whether I know the contents of the letter ?'

'I want to know the contents.'

'And suppose the contents were significant, just what would be the advantage to us in communicating them to you ?'

'You would have a valuable ally.'

'In this business,' Mason said, smiling, 'the difficult thing is to tell whether you're making an ally, or simply arming an enemy at your rear.'

'You have my word, Mr Mason . . . and I am very fond of Dorothy.'

Mason took from his pocket the copy of the letter which had been made on Dorothy Fenner's portable typewriter. Wordlessly, he handed it to Dorley Alder.

The older man all but grabbed at the letter in his eagerness. He started reading rapidly, his eyes shifting back and forth from line to line. When he had finished, he lowered the letter to his lap, sat for a moment gazing vacantly at the opposite wall of the office. Then he said softly, 'Good heavens.'

Mason gently reached forward and, taking advantage of Dorley Alder's preoccupied concentration, slipped the copy of the letter from the man's lap, folded it and put it back in his pocket.

'Good lord,' Dorley said, almost to himself, 'I had suspected something, but nothing like that – nothing at all like that.'

'It gave you a jolt?' Mason asked.

Dorley Alder said, 'George is a peculiar boy – a most peculiar boy, Mr Mason. The man will not permit anything to stand in his way. Once he makes up his mind to a certain course of conduct, I believe he would sacrifice his own life or the life of anyone else to carry out his purpose. Mr Mason, I must see the original of that letter.'

'I'm sorry, but that's impossible.'

'Why is it impossible?'

'A copy was made of the letter. The original letter then disappeared.'

Sudden anger suffused Dorley Alder's countenance. 'Good lord, Mr Mason, are you trying to play games like that with *me*?'

'I am telling you that this is a copy of the letter that was in that bottle.'

'Stuff and nonsense.'

'An exact copy,' Mason went on.

'How do you know it's an exact copy?'

'I can assure you that it is.'

Dorley Alder said, 'I'm afraid that you're either being victimised by your client, or that you're trying to victimise me. I . . . No, Mason, I'm sorry. That slipped out. I lost my self-control because I'm so bitterly disappointed. I was hoping you had that original letter in your possession or that your client did. I had every reason to believe such was the case.'

Mason said, 'This is a copy.'

'Who says so?'

'My client.'

'Poof!'

'And,' Mason went on, 'one other witness who compared it with the original, a witness whose name I'm not prepared to disclose at the moment.'

Dorley Alder's face lit up. 'You mean that there is a disinterested witness who can vouch for the accuracy of this copy?'

'Yes.'

'That,' Dorley Alder said, 'is different.'

'Quite different,' Mason assured him.

'Does George know that letter was copied?'

'I don't think so.'

'He may suspect it?'

'He may.'

'Did George manage to get that letter back?'

'There's every indication that he did.'

Dorley Alder sat in silent thought for several seconds, then he turned to Mason and said impressively, 'Mr Mason, I want you to keep away from George Alder. I want your client to keep away from George Alder. I am particularly concerned about her. If George has any idea that she has a copy of that letter she . . . well, in the interests of safety, in the interests of preserving her life, I feel that she should take steps to safeguard herself. She is in custody now, and . . .'

'She isn't any longer,' Mason said. 'She was released on bail about an hour ago.'

'She was?'

'That's right.'

'And where is she now?'

'At her apartment, I believe.'

Dorley Alder pushed his way up out of the depths of the big chair, said to Mason, 'Keep her away from George Alder. Stay away from George Alder yourself. Safeguard the copy of that letter. You may hear from me within the next day or two. Remember what I told you, Mr Mason. You have made a valuable ally.'

'Just a minute,' Mason said. 'There are two questions I should like to ask.'

'What are they?'

'How did you learn about that letter in the bottle?'

'Frankly, I learned as much as I knew from my nephew, George S. Alder. He started to confide in me, then changed his mind. I knew enough to know there had been such a letter.

'I wanted to find out more about it. I asked Dorothy if she had heard anything about it. She hadn't. I hoped my question would inspire her to make inquiries of Pete Cadiz.

'And your second question, Mr Mason?'

'Why are you so afraid of George?'

'I'm not.'

'But you've emphasised that I am not to go near him, and that . . .'

'Oh, that!'

'Yes, that.'

'Well, Mr Mason . . . I, personally, am not afraid of him. When he is crossed he has rages that are terrible. When Corrine disappeared in this fit of suicidal despondency, I fear it may have been caused in part by a difference of opinion she was having with him. He flew down to South America to get her to sign some papers. It is my understanding that she first turned him down, then refused to see him after that and . . . well, you know the rest. . . . Frankly I don't feel he ever forgave the poor sick girl for not yielding to his demands.

'However, I have answered this second question perhaps too fully. I must leave – at once.'

He bowed to Della Street, shook hands with Mason, turned towards the corridor door, said, 'I can get out this way?'

Mason nodded.

'Say nothing about my having been here,' Dorley Alder said, 'nothing to anyone.'

He strode to the exit door, opened it and walked out without once looking back, yet managing to maintain the dignity and power of his presence by the even set of his shoulders and the lines of his back.

Mason and his secretary were silent for some seconds after the door had closed.

'Well?' Della Street asked at length.

Mason said, 'Get Dorothy Fenner on the phone, Della. Tell her that I am anxious to have her keep away from George Alder, and for the moment not to be available to Dorley Alder.'

Della Street raised her eyebrows.

'Anything that Dorley has to say to her,' Mason explained, 'can be said through me. You may or may not have noticed it, Della, but the man was careful to say that *all* the shares of stock were in the trust.'

'And?' she asked.

'Carmen Monterrey is supposed to hold ten shares that aren't in the trust.'

Della Street thought that over. 'And could those ten shares be important?'

'They might be *damned* important, Della.'

68

'Then we didn't make an ally after all, Chief?'

'That,' Mason said, 'will be disclosed in due time.'

'And what's due time?'

'Damn soon,' he said, grinning.

CHAPTER EIGHT

The knock on the door of Dorothy Fenner's apartment was quietly insistent, and yet there was something almost apologetic in the gentle, steady, tat – tat – tat – tat – tat.

Dorothy Fenner walked to the door, jerked it open and said, irritably, 'I wish you newspaper people would telephone before you try storming the door. I've been . . .'

She stopped in startled dismay.

'May I come in?' George Alder asked.

Wordlessly, she stood to one side, holding the door open for him.

'The newspaper people have been here?' he asked.

She nodded.

'That's good,' he said.

'Sit down,' she invited.

'Lock the door, please.'

She hesitated an appreciable instant, then turned the knurled knob on the door, putting the bolt into place.

It was an old-fashioned apartment, with old-fashioned furniture, but there was a certain roominess about it, and the ceilings were high. Woodwork and furniture were dark, which by day made it gloomy and depressing, by night furnished an atmosphere of genteel respectability.

Alder said, 'All right, what are your terms?'

'What do you mean?' she asked.

Alder settled himself in the straight-backed chair near the table. There was something in his pose which made it seem he was on the point of pulling out cheque-book and fountain-pen.

'I made a fool of myself,' he admitted.

She watched him with outward hostility as her mind began adjusting itself to this new development.

'Why the sudden burst of conscience?' she asked.

He said, 'It isn't conscience, it's business.'

'Any business can be discussed with my lawyer, Perry Mason.'

'Don't be a fool!'

'What's foolish about that?'

'He's rich. He makes more every day than you do in a month.'

'What does that have to do with it?'

'I'm prepared to be decent and reasonable. All this newspaper notoriety has hurt you. You've probably lost your job. I'll compensate you for the damage I've caused, but there's no reason for *you* to pay Perry Mason part of *your* money.'

'You'll pay him?'

'Don't be a fool. I'm not that dumb. I might be willing to pay you for the damage to *you*. I'll be damned if I support a lawyer with any of my money.'

She had moved towards the telephone. Now she paused to think that over.

'You're a working girl,' he told her. 'You'd better start using your brain. You haven't done much with it so far.'

She walked back towards him and seated herself on the arm of the overstuffed chair, one arm over the back of the chair, the other indolently at her side, her right foot crossed over her left knee. A movie star being interviewed for one of the fan magazines had assumed this pose and it had been extremely effective. Dorothy Fenner had tried, liked it, and filed it away for future use. There was a certain nonchalance about it, an air of informal ease, and it didn't detract any from her looks.

'Let's quit beating around the bush and put a few cards on the table,' Alder said.

She said nothing, watching him with thoughtful speculation.

Alder said. 'If Minerva Danby wrote that letter, it's absolutely false. Frankly, I don't think she wrote it. I think it's a forgery. I think it's all either part of a hoax or a trap so that someone can lay the foundation for blackmail.'

Dorothy Fenner held her pose.

'However, when that bottle came into my possession and I read that astounding letter,' Alder went on 'I wanted time to think, and I wanted time to investigate. I started an inquiry on that Los Merritos thing. It's absolutely false from beginning to end. And I want you to believe me, that I *didn't* see Minerva Danby at all that night. In fact, I simply can't account for that letter.'

He was talking earnestly now, apparently really trying to convince her. Dorothy Fenner had sense enough to realise that silence had so far been her best move. She merely watched him, letting

70

him see she was listening, afraid to say anything lest he find out the cards she held were not as high as he had feared – interested now in just how far the man would go, just what sort of a proposition he was prepared to make. After all there could be no harm in listening. She could always call Perry Mason *after* she had heard what Alder had to say.

'It's the truth,' Alder said, pleading with her now for her belief. 'I was detained in town. I had intended to shove off about eight o'clock that night, but I didn't get down to the yacht until after eleven. I gave the captain orders to shove off and I didn't check the weather or pay very much attention to it.

'About half an hour out, one of those terrific wind-storms came swooping down and caught us out in the middle of everything. It was quite a blow. I was on the bridge with the captain nearly all night. I asked him about Minerva Danby. He said she was in one of the staterooms and had gone to bed.

'Well, you know what happened. In the morning, I waited for her to join me at breakfast. When she didn't show up, I sent the steward to her room. The room was empty, the bed hadn't been slept in. I thought for a while she might have gone ashore, but the crew told me she hadn't left the yacht. It had been a terribly rough passage going over, and we'd taken a bit of water, nothing too serious, but we'd had a few of them come over the lower deck. However, you couldn't possibly think that she could have washed overboard, and there doesn't seem to be any reason for thinking it could have been well, anything else.'

'You mean murder?' Dorothy Fenner asked calmly.

He jerked himself more erect in the chair. His eyed rebuked her. 'Certainly not. I meant suicide. Don't talk that way Dorothy.'

'I see,' she said.

'However,' he went on, 'her body was found, and the autopsy showed death by drowning in salt water, and that was that.

'Then, after all this time, Pete Cadiz rings me up to tell me he has a letter that had been tossed overboard from the *Thayerbelle*. I didn't think anything of it, thought it must have been some prank, but since he'd gone to the trouble of ringing me up I told him to bring it in and I'd pay him for the trip, and . . . well, there I was, caught flat-footed.

'I didn't know what to do. I'm about to launch an investigation – or I was. And then you came in and stole the letter. You can realise the position in which that put me. If that letter had been published in the papers . . . well, I lost my head, I guess. You see,

71

the guests had seen you jumping out of the window with something in your hand. They insisted that I should look and see what was gone, and that I must notify the police.

'I was desperately afraid that the police might catch you and find that bottle in your possession and yet I had no alternative. I couldn't simply sit back and say, "Oh, it doesn't amount to anything. Whoever it was was probably looking for a few postage stamps, or something of that sort." Hang it, I was in a position where I *had* to call the police.

'But first, of course, we tried to run you down. By the time we spotted that canoe, I had a pretty good idea what must have happened, and when we went down through the yacht anchorage and I saw your yacht there, I felt certain.

'I had to make up some story for the police, so I pulled the one about the gems, thinking I could perhaps work things out afterwards.'

'You got the letter back?' she asked.

His face was grim. 'You can thank your lucky stars that I got that letter back. Otherwise you might not have been alive the next morning. I am not accustomed to being pushed around, my dear – and on this matter my reputation is at stake.'

She tried to keep fear from her eyes. 'What do you want?'

'Only to know who your accomplice was, how you learned of the letter, and to ensure your silence – by some of the more satisfactory means which are available – satisfactory to you, I mean.'

His smile was ingratiating, but his eyes were cold and deadly.

'How did you know where I hid the bottle?'

He laughed. 'The most simple of all places, my dear. During prohibition, we yachtsmen always hid our liquor in the fresh-water tanks.'

'With the letter back, you didn't have to turn me in to the police.'

'I didn't turn *you* in. I merely complained of a thief – which I simply had to do. I had no idea that the police could actually find anything that would lead to you. I thought you'd be too smart for that.'

He said that last reproachfully and she, flaring to her own defence, said, 'It was that dog of yours.'

'I admit that was a mistake,' he said. 'I shudder to think what would have happened if he'd caught you.'

'Well, that's the reason I had to abandon that bath towel,' she said.

'There were too many witnesses to the burglary. I couldn't

back up after I'd called the police. I had to go ahead. And that damn lawyer of yours! Why in the world did you ever get Perry Mason, of all people?'

'What's wrong with *him*?'

'He's too damned clever.'

'That's why I got him.'

'Well, he certainly crucified me this afternoon. Of course, those damned jewels. . . . I didn't realise at the time they were all covered by insurance, but then as soon as Mason started asking me about the insurance I knew I was licked. If I made a claim that the gems were lost, the insurance company would start an independent investigation, and – well, I was just licked, and that's all there was to it. If I don't make a claim against the insurance company, it's going to be a give-away, and if I do, it'll be trying to get money by false pretences. Insurance companies don't take kindly to that.'

'What happened this afternoon?' she asked, sparring for time.

'That deputy district attorney got hold of me after court, and told me he didn't like my answers, and that he would have to dismiss the case if I couldn't be more co-operative. So I pushed back my chair, managed to put on quite an act, told him I was entitled to more consideration as a taxpayer, but that as far as I was concerned, he could go ahead and dismiss the case; that I'd seen enough of his court-room tactics to know that Perry Mason would tie him up in a knot and make me a laughing-stock instead of an aggrieved victim, so I didn't give a damn. Then I turned and stalked out of the office.'

'And now?' he said, 'I want to come to terms.'

'What terms?'. .

'As a business man, I suppose I should say that I want to do what's right and then try to keep the figure at the lowest possible point. But I don't feel much like a business man now. I feel like a parent, perhaps an uncle who has harmed someone whom he really loves. . . . How much?'

'For what?'

He held up his hands as he checked off the points. 'For a complete release; for complete silence on your part as far as the Press is concerned; for the name of your accomplice; and for completely forgetting that letter.'

'I don't think I could do that. I don't think it's fair. And I really didn't have an accomplice. I just happened to be picked up by a casual canoeist.'

He studied her, and she felt uneasy under his eyes. 'The letter,' he said impressively, 'is a forgery. You have my assurance of that. Will that make it any easier for you to promise to forget?'

'How do I know it's a forgery?'

'I'll *prove* it to you.'

'Go ahead.'

'Not here. I haven't even the letter here, much less the proof. But if you'll give me the chance, my dear, I'll *prove* the forgery, the complete spuriousness of that letter. Then there will be nothing to prevent you being reasonable with me.'

She thought over what he had said, her eyes speculative. 'And you'd give me money?'

'Of course, my dear, a large . . . well, shall we say an adequate sum? After all, Dorothy, while you and I don't get along, I'm trustworthy.'

She turned her eyes to get away from his probing scrutiny. The telephone caught and held her gaze.

George Alder said, 'Look, you're nervous, you're upset, and you're a little frightened of me, aren't you?'

'I think you have some ulterior motive, or you wouldn't be . . .'

'Good lord!' he exclaimed impatiently. 'I don't want notoriety. And I'm trying to do the right thing – if you'll only let me.'

He got to his feet.

'Dorothy,' he said 'I'm going back to the island. You think this over. Then, when you've seen the logic of my position, when you're ready to accept a very adequate cash payment and be relieved of this criminal prosecution, you will come to me and I'll prove to you that this letter is a complete falsification.'

'When?'

'Any time tonight, dear. The sooner the better. I'll let the servants go and the dog will be shut up in his closet. I'll be waiting.'

'Not tonight. I . . .'

'Tonight,' he interrupted with firm insistence. 'I have plans of my own to make. And remember, my dear, you're still guilty of breaking and entering, and even though you're out on bail, you're still the defendant in a criminal action. *Say nothing to anyone.* Just come and let me show you the real proof of the falsity of the charges made in that letter, and then you and I will come to a complete understanding.

'I'll be waiting, my dear, but say nothing to anyone. And it would be better if you left this hotel – shall we say, surreptitiously? Your lawyer, you know, would want to have a hand in this settlement, and we don't want him to have any of *your* money. Do we, Dorothy?'

He walked rapidly to the door, paused in the doorway, and said, 'Remember, I'll be there at the island – waiting. The dog will be shut up and the servants absent. Just walk across the bridge and then around the walk to my study door. You know the way.

'Good night, Dorothy.'

He closed the door behind him.

CHAPTER NINE

Paul Drake, seated in his cubbyhole of a private office, a green plastic eyeshade pulled down over his eyes, studied a series of reports. Telephones on his desk kept him constantly in touch with the men who were out in the field. On the wall an electric clock silently paced the seconds.

Perry Mason and Della Street, using the prerogative of long friendship and the relationship of steady employers, marched unannounced down the narrow corridor, tapped perfunctorily on the door of Drake's private office, and then Mason held it open so that Della Street could enter first.

Drake looked up from his reports, grinned, glanced at the clock, rubbed his eyes, and said, 'I was just getting ready to knock off and go home. Where have you folks been?'

Mason slipped his arm around Della Street's waist. 'Dining, dancing and relaxing, Paul. At this stage we're hiring you to do the work.'

Drake said wearily, 'Maybe you think it *isn't* work! These birds who think a private detective has glamorous adventures, plays tag with cops, spends his free time fighting off beautiful babes, should try keeping two dozen operatives working so they get results and don't fall all over each other's feet.'

'What's new?' Mason asked.

'Lot's of things. Nothing startling, just a lot of details that we can button up into a package by morning. Things always slow down a little around this time of night. You can't get people to talk after they've gone to bed, no matter how many men you have on the job, so I usually start laying men off, and plan on an early morning start.'

'You find out anything about Corrine?' Mason asked.

'Evidently she was despondent because a close friend had walked out on her. That friend, incidentally, was Minerva Danby who was washed overboard from George Alder's yacht.

'George Alder flew to South America when he heard his half sister was mentally sick. He arrived the day she disappeared. Circumstances indicate suicide over despondency, but her body was never found.

'Carmen Monterrey, Corrine's maid and companion, is back in this country somewhere. I've put ads in all the papers – routine wording: 'If Carmen Monterrey will communicate with the undersigned, she'll learn something very much to her advantage," I've had a blind box number on the ad, so . . .'

The right-hand phone on Drake's desk rang insistently.

The detective motioned excuses to Mason, picked up the telephone, said, 'Hello . . . Okay, go ahead . . . What? . . . The hell! . . . Okay, give me details . . . All right, get details and feed them in here just as fast as you can. I'm sending a couple more men down to help you get the dope. I want facts . . . All right, I'll be right here . . . you start digging. I'll have two men down there within half an hour . . . All right, get them.'

Drake slammed up the phone, said, 'Just a minute, Perry, hold everything.'

He grabbed the phone on his left and barked an order to someone in the office. 'Get two men down to the Alder residence on the island. I want them to help Jake. Get them started fast . . . No, I don't care what two men you take. This takes precedence over everything . . . only get *good* men. This is hot!'

Drake dropped the receiver into place, pushed the green eye-shade up on his forehead and said, 'George Alder's been murdered.'

'The devil he has! When?'

'Apparently within the last few hours. Sally Bangor, employed as a servant, made the discovery, and surprised the murderer red-handed in the study. Death apparently by gunshot. Body lying sprawled out on the floor of his study. Outer door open. Dog inside a converted closet where George kept him shut up when he was expecting visitors.

'The man I had assigned to keep the house covered just got there. He found police cars around the place, got a flash that Alder had been murdered, and beat it to a phone to give me the news. Now he's gone back to prowl around and contact someone who will talk – a newspaper photographer, reporter, friendly cop, or someone. He has contacts and we should hear from him in a few minutes.'

'Why didn't you have him on the job before this?' Mason asked irritably.

'Have a heart, Perry. There was no indication there was anything *urgent* about covering the house. In fact, I debated whether to put anyone on there before morning. I . . .'

'It's all right, Paul,' Mason interrupted. 'I'm jumpy.'

Drake said, 'Excuse me a minute and I'll go out to the switchboard and start directing activities from there. I can gain a little time that way and I may be able to pick up some stuff from one of the newspaper offices here.'

Drake left the room and Mason exchanged glances with Della Street, then started pacing the floor.

Della Street sat motionless, watching him, her shorthand notebook poised on her knee, a pencil held over it, ready to take down any instructions Mason might give. But the lawyer continued to pace thoughtfully back and forth across the narrow confines of Drake's office, his chin on his chest.

After some ten or fifteen minutes, Drake came bustling back into the room and said, 'I have a whole flock of lines out, Perry, but it'll take me a while to get details. Want to wait or get 'em in the morning?'

Mason grinned, perched himself on the one uncluttered corner of Drake's desk and said, 'Foolish question . . . we'll wait.'

Drake pulled out a package of cigarettes from his desk drawer, made a gesture of invitation to Della Street, who shook her head, and to Mason, who said, 'Thanks, Paul, I have one of my own.'

Mason opened his cigarette-case and he and Drake lit up.

'This is the sort of stuff that drives you nuts in this business,' Drake said. 'I have two dozen men on the job. It gets around to the slack time and I start calling them in. Then something like this breaks. I'm like a runner with too short a lead off first base with the batter rapping out a short single. I'm falling over myself trying to get started.'

'If you feel that way about it,' Mason said, 'think about me.'

Drake shook his head. 'Your job hasn't started yet. I'm getting you the facts. After I get them, you can take whatever action is indicated – probably nothing, now that the guy's been murdered.'

Mason glanced at Della Street, grinned and said, 'Listen to the detective telling the lawyer how easy the life of an attorney is.'

Drake said, 'You think a detective has a cinch. Remember I have a reputation. I'm supposed to get you the facts all wrapped up in a neat package so you can go to work on them. Tell me, Perry, what will this thing do? Will it close out your interest in the case?'

'I don't think so,' Mason said. 'I'm gunning for bigger stakes.'

Drake glanced at him, raised an inquiring eyebrow, but didn't put the question into words.

Della Street picked up the evening paper that was on the floor beside the chair she occupied and started reading.

Mason said, 'I hate to hold out on you, Paul.'

'It's okay,' Drake said. Sometimes I can be of a little more help if I know what you're working on, that's all. From where I sit, it looks as though Dorothy Fenner was out in the clear right now. The DA won't be able to prosecute without someone to swear that certain specific property is missing. From all I can hear, you gave Alder quite a going over in the court-room this afternoon.'

Mason said, 'There's more to it than Dorothy Fenner's case, Paul.'

'Yeah, I know,' Drake said. 'That's what I gathered.'

Mason said, 'This has to be in strict confidence, Paul.'

'I've never let you down yet, have I?'

'Nope,' Mason said, 'but when you take a look at this, you'll see that it's loaded with dynamite.'

Mason took from his pocket the copy of the letter which had been contained in the bottle and passed it over to Paul Drake. 'Take a look at that, Paul.'

Drake read the letter, at first with nervous impatience, his eyes on the sheet of paper, but his ears listening for the telephones. Then suddenly he snapped his attention to sharp focus on the letter, and muttered half under his breath, 'For the love of Mike!'

'Some dynamite, eh, Paul?'

Drake didn't answer. He remained utterly engrossed in the letter.

Della Street looked up from the newspaper, started to say something, then folded the paper and waited until Drake had finished reading.

Mason adjusted himself to a more comfortable position, interlaced his fingers over his knee-cap.

One of the telephones rang.

Drake, with his eyes still on the letter, groped absently for the telephone.

With swift efficiency, Della Street picked up the phone and put it in Drake's groping hand.

'Thanks,' Drake said. Then, into the telephone, 'Yes, hello?'

He listened to words which came rattling from the receiver, said, 'Well, that's a *lot* better! Give me some more facts.'

He listened for a few seconds, then put down the letter he was reading, picked up a pencil, and started making notes.

'That all?' he asked.

He listened to some more talk on the receiver, said, 'Okay, I think you're doing good. Now, you'll have help down there in just a little while. I want to get all the facts I can and I want to find out what the police are doing. I'll be sitting right here. Keep feeding in the facts.

'Good lord, Perry,' Drake said, 'that letter is *really* something. Where did you get it?'

Mason said, 'Apparently it was found in a bottle that had drifted ashore and was picked up by a beachcomber who turned the thing over to Alder. Now, that'll show you something of what I have in mind. What did you learn just now, anything new?'

'Looks like a real break for your client,' Drake said.

'Shoot.'

'That is,' Drake went on, 'unless Dorothy Fenner went back to Alder's house to finish the job she started Saturday night.'

'Don't be silly,' Mason told him. 'Dorothy Fenner is a good little girl, She's following my instructions. I took her home, and she's staying at home.'

'How do you know?'

'I told her what to do. I think she has enough confidence in me to do exactly what I told her. What have you found out, Paul?'

Drake said, 'That was my man down at Alder's place. He contacted a deputy sheriff who gave him all the dope. It looks as though the same prowler that was down there Saturday night came back and went to work again. This time she didn't jump out of the window. The dog was shut up in the closet and when Alder surprised her, she gave him the works with a thirty-eight-calibre double-action revolver.'

'What makes them think it's the same one?' Mason asked, his eyes narrowing.

'Because of what police refer to as *modus operandi*, the person who was in the study ran out through open french windows at the back of the study. These french windows open on the bay side. Sally Bangor, the servant who made the discovery of the body, had enough presence of mind to close the gate across the bridge when she ran back to the mainland. That left the murderer marooned on the island.

'The maid's screams got action from a passing motorist, and radio cops were on the job within a matter of minutes. When they heard Sally Bangor's story they drew their guns and started making a routine search of the premises, leaving a committee of curious citizens who had gathered to stand at the mainland end of the bridge and see that no one doubled back behind them and got off the island that way.'

'And ?' Mason asked.

'And they found precisely nothing,' Drake said, 'no sign of the murderer. The only way that the murderer *could* have escaped was by water, just as she did the other night.'

'What's the rest of it ?' Mason asked.

'Well, George Alder was lying face down in a huge pool of blood. He'd been shot through the neck with a thirty-eight-calibre revolver, and the bullet had severed one of the big arteries, gone clean on through the neck and apparently didn't lodge anywhere in the room. That gives police the line of fire. The woman who shot him must have been standing right by the desk. Alder apparently fell in his tracks.'

'How do the police figure she was standing by the desk ?'

'Because only in that case could the bullet have gone through Alder's neck and then out through the open french doors. Alder pitched forward. The girl must have thrown the gun at him as he fell.'

'How come ?'

'The gun was found *under* the body, all crusted with blood, and one shell fired. So there they have things in a nutshell, Perry.'

'Where was the dog all this time ?'

'Locked up in a closet where apparently he stays most of the time when Alder is entertaining visitors in his study. The dog is rather unsocial. He's been trained as a combat dog . . . not the type that does much barking, but the kind that goes into action. He had the regular Army training, pursuing people, dragging them down, and all that stuff.

'As I understand it, if a person stands perfectly still with his hands up in the air, the dog is trained to crouch and not do anything, but the minute the person moves or assumes a threatening gesture, the dog will tear him apart.'

'And what was the dog doing all the time the murder was taking place?'

Paul Drake looked completely blank. 'How the dickens – Oh, I see. I'll get my man to look into it and let you know later.'

Mason said, 'How long ago did all this take place, Paul?'

Drake said, 'As nearly as police can tell from a superficial examination, the murder must have taken place around nine o'clock this evening. It was the servant's night out and she didn't return until around ten o'clock.'

'So the murder must have been in there searching for an hour?'

'Apparently so.'

Mason looked at his watch. 'Hell, Paul, it's twelve o'clock now.'

'I told you,' Drake said, 'that I probably made a slip-up by not having a man down there covering the house sooner. As it was, I sent this fellow down, told him to go on duty at midnight and keep the place under observation until eight in the morning, when I'd have a relief for him. Gosh, Perry, you wanted dope on Alder, but you didn't want anybody tailed, and I even debated with myself whether to put anyone on watch at the house or not, but finally decided I'd do it just to get the licence number of cars that might drive up, and . . .'

'It's all right,' Mason said. 'I think I'll go get Dorothy Fenner out of bed and tell her about it. That may forestall some interviews with the newspaper, and . . .'

Della Street, who had been waiting for a break in the conversation, said, 'Before you go, Chief, you might take a look at this.'

'What?'

Della Street raised the paper and said, 'Here's a want ad: "If Carmen Monterrey, who was in South America nine months ago, will communicate with the undersigned, she will receive information to her financial advantage. Box 123J." '

'Sure,' Drake, 'that's the ad I put in the paper.'

'And how did you get it in the *afternoon* paper?' Della Street asked.

Drake suddenly jerked upright to startled attention. 'What?' he yelled. 'Let me have that paper.'

Mason said, 'Looks as though someone might be one jump ahead of us, Paul. Better try and find out if you can what that Box 123J is. Della, get yourself a taxi and go on home and try and get some sleep. I'm going down, get Dorothy Fenner out of bed, and beat the police to the punch.'

'Think they'll call on her?' Drake asked.

'Oh sure,' Mason said, 'unless they have already. However, I'll have a nice little heart-to-heart talk.'

'You don't want me with you?' Della Street asked, somewhat wistfully.

'No. You go get some sleep.'

'Gosh, I don't feel as if I *ever* wanted to sleep.'

'Take a pill,' Mason advised. 'You're going to have to be on the job in the morning.'

'But how about you?' she asked.

'I,' Mason said, somewhat grimly, 'am going to have to get on the job right now.'

CHAPTER TEN

The Monadnock Hotel Apartments had an ornate front which made an imposing impression of glittering white stucco and red tile. The sides of the building were plain uncovered brick, with narrow windows indicating that most of the apartments were spaced in the conventional cramped intervals required by tenants in the lower economic brackets.

Mason parked his car, ran up the front steps, entered the long, narrow lobby, saw the light over the desk, and approached the night clerk.

'You have a Dorothy Fenner living here,' he said. I'm Perry Mason.'

The clerk ostentatiously looked at the clock.

'Her lawyer,' Mason said. 'Ring her, please and tell her I'm here.'

The clerk plugged in the line, depressed a key several times, then said, 'I'm afraid she doesn't care to answer, or . . . oh, just a minute.'

Into the mouthpiece he said, 'Mr Perry Mason, your attorney, wishes to see you.'

He hesitated a moment, frowned, once more looked at the clock, then said to Mason, rather dubiously, 'You may go up, Mr Mason. It's Apartment 459.'

Mason took the elevator to the fourth floor, followed the numbers of the apartments down the corridor, tapped on the door of 459.

Dorothy Fenner, attired in a housecoat, opened the door and said, 'Why, Mr Mason.'

Mason said, 'Sorry, I have to see you.'

She stood to one side, swinging the door open for him to come in, then closed it behind him.

She said, 'The apartment's a mess. It's a single and – well, there's the bed down and – I was sound asleep. I am hardly awake yet.'

'Okay,' Mason told her. 'Let's do some fast talking. George Alder is dead.'

'Dead!'

Mason nodded.

'How in the world. Why . . . what happened?'

'Murdered.'

'Good heavens! Who killed him? What . . .'

'They don't know,' Mason said. 'A preliminary report states that Sally Bangor, a servant, found his body lying on the floor when she returned from her evening off.'

'Sally Bangor!'

'You know her?' Mason asked.

'I know who she is, yes. I've been at the house as a guest several times.'

Mason said, 'Well, the police *may* come here to question you.'

'Why?'

'Because of what happened Saturday night.'

'What does that have to do with it?'

'Nothing,' Mason said, 'except that there's some indication the person who committed the murder escaped by water. The police may decide they'll put two and two together. Have you been out anywhere tonight?'

'No, I've been in my room ever since I was released.'

'How about dinner?'

'I didn't want any. I just fixed myself a cup of chocolate and let it go at that. I had all the materials here so I didn't go out.'

'Any proof of that?'

She said irritably, 'A single woman is hardly in a position to furnish an alibi for the time she's in bed.'

'I mean during the evening. Anyone know that you didn't go out?'

'Why, of course, the man at the desk would have seen me if I'd gone out.'

Mason sat down on the edge of the bed. Dorothy Fenner came over and sat down beside him.

83

'Alder didn't try to telephone you or get in communication with you, did he?' Mason asked, ' – after court, I mean.'

She crossed her knees. The housecoat fell away from her right leg. She gathered the garment, started to draw it into place, then regarded her flesh contemplatively and said, 'You know, Mr Mason, for an office girl, I really have a nice sunburn, haven't I?'

She stretched the leg out, and moved the housecoat up so that he could see the bronzed blonde skin.

Mason gave her leg a casual glance, nodded, said, 'Nice.'

'Thank you.'

'We were talking about George Alder,' Mason reminded her.

'Oh, yes, what about him?'

'Whether he telephoned or tried to get in touch with you.'

She touched her bare leg at about the place where the top of her stocking would have been, moved her fingers along it slowly as though tracing some invisible line.

Mason said, 'For heaven sakes wake up, pay attention to me. Let's get this stuff over with. Answer the question, can't you? It would seem that you are deliberately trying to distract my attention in order to gain time.'

She deliberated for two or three seconds, then said, quietly, 'He was here.'

'Here!' Mason exclaimed.

'Yes.'

'The deuce he was. When?'

'I presume after he'd finished a conference with the deputy district attorney, and before he went back home.'

'Can you fix the time?'

'Oh, I'd say somewhere around six or half past.'

Mason said, 'Now look, this hearing was in an adjoining county. After I secured your discharge I drove you back here. That took forty minutes. Now, how long after you arrived here at this apartment hotel, and I had let you out of the car at the kerb, did Alder get here?'

'Oh, I'd say it was an hour. Perhaps a little over.'

'And during that time he'd been closeted with the district attorney down there?'

'Some of the time, yes. At least that's what he said.'

'Why didn't he go directly back to his island home? Why did he come all the way here?'

'He wanted to see me.'

'What did he want?'

84

'He was holding out an olive branch. He said he wanted to make some sort of a settlement.'

'Why didn't you notify me?'

Here eyes were wide with innocence. 'Why, I was going to — first thing in the morning.'

'But why didn't you let me know immediately?'

'You said you could only be reached through this Drake Detective Agency and not to call you unless it was something *extremely* urgent. I thought that could wait until tomorrow.'

'What was his idea of a settlement?'

'He wanted to pay me some money, I know that.'

'How much?'

'He was indefinite.'

She had extended her right forefinger now and was tracing intricate patterns on the flesh of her leg.

'Go ahead, what happened?'

'He suggested that he'd acted hastily. He admitted that he had gone out to my yacht, searched it, found the bottle and taken possession of that letter again. He said he could prove to me the letter was a forgery and said he wanted to make some sort of adjustment for the trouble I'd been to.'

'And you didn't call me?'

'Why, I thought that could keep until morning.'

'And just what did he want you to do?'

'Just make a settlement.'

'Did he offer you any amount?'

'Nothing specific, but he said that if I'd come down to his house he could first prove to me that the letter was a forgery, and then . . .'

'When?'

'When I got there.'

'No, no. I mean when did he want you to come?'

'Tonight, or . . . What time is it? . . . Oh, it's morning. Well then, it was last night.'

'What else did he say?'

'He said he'd be expecting me, that he'd leave the gate unlocked across the bridge and the gate in the wall unlocked. I could open both gates and walk right around to the side of the house where I was to go directly into his study. He said he'd have the dog shut up and he'd be waiting for me.'

'You didn't go?'

'Of course not. You told me not to.'

'But you didn't tell him you weren't coming?'

'No.'

'Why?'

'I thought I'd better keep your instructions to myself.'

'To whom have you said anything about this conversation?'

'To no one.'

'You're certain you didn't go?'

'Of course I didn't go. Naturally I didn't want to see him unless you were along.'

'And exactly what did he want?'

'He wanted my promise that we'd never say anything about that letter to the newspapers. He said he could convince both of us that it was all a fraud, a pack of false statements.'

Mason got up off the edge of the bed and began pacing the floor. 'You haven't told anyone about this?'

'No.'

'Don't.'

'Why not?'

Mason said, 'Don't be silly. They'd try to hang the murder on you then. They know that Alder was expecting someone and the assumption is that the person was responsible for his murder. If they found out Alder was expecting *you* they'd . . .'

'But I had no intention in the world of going down there. He kept insisting that he'd keep the gates and door open for me, and that the dog would be chained up.'

'The dog was shut up in a closet,' Mason said.

'I think he keeps the dog there much of the time when he's expecting people around the house, doesn't he?'

'I guess so. How do you get along with the dog?'

'I've virtually never seen him except that Saturday night when he came running after me. Whenever I've been there as a guest the dog has been shut up in that sort of closet. It's really a little dog apartment, and Prince is quite happy there.'

'What kind of a deal did Alder want to make with you?'

'I don't know. I told him he'd have to negotiate it with my lawyer.'

'So he may have been expecting *you* down there tonight?'

'Of course. He *wanted* me to come, but I told him that I wouldn't.'

'Did he take that answer as final?'

'He seemed to think he could hypnotise me, or browbeat me, or coax me into coming. Almost the last thing he said was that he'd be waiting there for me and that the gates would be left unlocked. I was to come right on into his study.'

Mason said, 'Don't tell anybody that. If the police come here, and it begins to look now as though they might, simply tell them that I was the one who told you George Alder was murdered. Explain to them that I came here especially to tell you not to make any statements to the police or to newspapers or to anyone, because technically your case is still pending in the courts. Use that as an excuse to keep from talking. Don't make *any* statements whatever other than, "no comment".'

She nodded.

'Think you can do that?'

'But yes, of course.'

Mason said, 'I don't want you to lie about anything, but I don't want you to tell anyone Alder was here tonight. And definitely, positively, absolutely, and finally, I don't want you, even by admission, intimation or otherwise to let anyone know that Alder had asked you to come down there tonight.'

'But won't I have to tell that sooner or later? Isn't it evidence, and . . .'

'You can tell it as evidence and at the proper time – if you have to,' Mason said. 'In the meantime we're going to watch and see what develops. You know Carmen Monterrey?'

'Of course.'

'You didn't put an ad for her in the paper, did you?'

'Me?'

'Yes.'

'Heavens, I haven't heard from her for weeks. She was down in South America and . . . well, I guess she stayed there for quite a while, hoping that there'd be some trace of Corrine. She was very much attached to Corrine, and I know she felt bitter against Minerva Danby because of the way Minerva Danby walked out. Well, after reading that letter, I don't know as I blame Minerva – I'd always felt rather bitter towards her from what I'd understood from Carmen's letters, and then – well, I can see now how it was from Minerva's standpoint. I think Carmen came back once when it seemed that Corrine might be here in this country, but it turned out to be a false lead and she went right back to South America. I don't know where she is now.'

Mason nodded, said, 'Don't try to pull any fancy stuff with the police. Get dressed, tell them I've been here, told you Alder was murdered and that you were not to give any interviews to the

Press or make any statements to the police, other than to state that you hadn't left this apartment since you returned to it around five-thirty or six o'clock.'

'But when they ask me how *you* knew about the murder what shall I tell them?'

Mason grinned, and said, 'Tell them you employ a lawyer to answer questions for you, that you don't want to start answering his questions for him. Okay?'

'Okay,' she said, smiling.

Mason picked up his hat, started for the door.

She came over to stand with her hand on the door-knob.

'You're nice.'

'Thanks.'

Abruptly she raised her lips. 'Good night,' she said.

As Mason bent to kiss her, her arm moved up around his neck, then her fingers were at the back of his head pulling the hair, pressing his head down to hers.

Then suddenly she released her hold, stepped back and looked at him with eyes that were dark with emotion.

'You *are* nice,' she half whispered.

'Thank you,' Mason said, and slipped out into the corridor.

It was two or three seconds before he heard the door close behind him and he had taken three more steps before he heard the bolt shoot angrily into place.

CHAPTER ELEVEN

When Perry Mason entered his office at nine-thirty on Tuesday morning Della Street said, 'Dorley Alder is out there.'

'What's new?'

'Drake has a report here – a lot of stuff – mostly an elaboration of what he told you last night.'

'That's fine. Give me a résumé and then I'll see Dorley Alder.'

'Apparently the dog was raising Cain at the time of the murder,' Della said, 'but when the police got there, the dog was lying quiet in the closet. The maid said that the dog had been trained to lie there, and when he was shut up in the closet he knew that was where he was supposed to stay.

'Police thought the murderer might still be on the island, or hiding in the house somewhere, and they wanted to use the dog to track her down. They asked the maid if she could control the dog, and the maid said she didn't think so and wasn't anxious to try. She said the dog had been fairly friendly with her, but that no one except George Alder was permitted to feed or go near it, and while the dog would tolerate her while Alder was around, the dog was always shut up when Alder wasn't there, and she didn't want any part of the animal.'

'And the dog was quiet all this time?'

'You mean while the police were moving around?'

'Yes.'

'That's the way I understand it from Drake's report.' Della said.

'And how did they know he'd been raising Cain when the murder was committed?'

'Well,' Della said, 'the police finally decided to open the door a crack, hold a rope with a noose in it, get the dog out of there and see if perhaps the maid could make him track down the person who had committed the murder. In the event the dog wasn't tractable, they'd have the rope around his neck.

'So, they opened the closet door, the dog lunged against the opening, came through like a shot, knocked one of the policemen over and tore out of the house, running nose to the ground.'

'And trailed the murderer?' Mason asked, interested.

'No,' said Della. 'He tried to get away, ran to the closed gate in the bridge, and started scratching, trying to get out through the gate.'

Mason said, 'That would be a pretty good indication the murderer had gone that way, Della.'

'Apparently she couldn't have. The servant ran out and closed the gate behind her, and was absolutely certain that no one crossed the bridge, nor could anyone have swum from the mainland across to the island. There's a sheer brick wall on both sides.'

Mason frowned thoughtfully.

'Now then, getting back to the way they know the dog was raising Cain when the murder was committed,' Della said. 'When the police looked inside the closet, they found that the door was all scratched up and blood streaks on the door indicated the dog must have torn one of his claws loose trying to get out. He probably went into a frenzy when he realised his master was in danger.'

'The dog hadn't clawed the door before?' Mason asked, interested.

'Never. The maid said that this closet had been fixed up as the dog's own. There was a mattress in there, a pan of water, and all the dog trappings. And of course there was ventilation which came in from a high window that was heavily barred. The dog had learned to stay in there quietly when he was put in there. Now, then, that's the story. You'd better see Mr Alder.'

She started for the doorway to bring Dorley Alder into the office, then paused. 'Did you see your client last night ?'

'Uh-huh.'

'Everything under control ?'

'Everything except the client.'

'How come ?'

'She was very grateful for all I was doing for her.'

'She should be grateful.'

'She had been in bed,' Mason said. 'She put on a housecoat.'

'And then ?' Della Street asked.

'Then,' Mason said, 'she commented on how brown her leg was, pointing out to me what a nice sun tan she'd managed to get despite the fact she was a working girl. It sounded like a stall.'

'Well, what of it ?' Della Street asked. 'Didn't she have a right to be proud of her sun tan ?'

'And when I left,' Mason went on, 'she came over to hold the door open for me and her good night was slightly more affectionate than I had anticipated.'

Della Street laughed. 'Perhaps the poor gal thinks she can use some influence to determine the amount of your fee.'

'It's a legitimate deduction from all the circumstances.' Mason said.

'You mean a deduction from the facts, or a deduction from the fee ?'

He said. 'You're too sharp for me this morning. Did you sleep ?'

'After two aspirin and two hours of tossing.'

'Drake hasn't found anything of Carmen Monterrey, has he ?'

'Not yet. He did find out something though that he's not supposed to know. He can't tell us how he learned it – through some contacts of his.'

'What ?'

'The Box 123J. That was George S. Alder.'

Mason paused to think that over, then nodded thoughtfully. 'Of course. That was Alder's logical move. He realised what he was up against as soon as he saw this letter in the bottle. He knew that he had to find Carmen. And perhaps through her find some way of discrediting some of Minerva Danby's statements. Okay, Della, go bring Dorley Alder in and we'll see what *he* wants.'

Dorley Alder entered the office as Della Street held the door open. He wasted no time in preliminaries. 'Mason, this is a damn bad business.'

'It is for a fact.'

Alder said, 'My nephew was a bachelor and apparently I'm the next of kin upon whom the responsibilities fall in such a case.'

Mason nodded, keeping his face without expression.

Dorley Alder seated himself in the big client's chair and said, 'What will happen with this case against Dorothy Fenner now, Mr Mason?'

'I presume it'll be dismissed. There won't be any complaining witness, no one to testify what, if any, articles were missing.'

Dorley said, 'Has it ever occurred to you, Mr Mason, that the authorities *might* try to implicate Dorothy Fenner in the murder?'

'It's a possibility,' Mason said, his voice showing casual unconcern. 'We're dealing with a county sheriff, of course – and anything may happen. However, if they try to throw suspicion on the Fenner girl they'll wind up by making themselves ludicrous.'

Dorley Alder took a leather-backed notebook from his pocket, said, 'I told you that you'd made an ally. I'll now prove it. The gun with which my nephew was shot was his own gun.'

'The devil it was!'

'That's right, one of the new Smith and Wessons with a two-inch barrel, a .38 special.'

'You're certain?'

'Quite. Not only have I checked the invoice where he purchased the gun, but the weapon was evidently one he was carrying on his person at the time of his death. The sheriff, I believe, is trying at the moment to keep this information from the Press.'

'It could very well have been suicide then?'

'I'm not prepared to state. There are, I believe, such matters as powder tattooing to be taken into consideration. A technical expert has given it as his *opinion* that the gun must have been too far away for the wound to have been self-inflicted.'

'But the gun had been fired?' Mason asked.

'Not only had one shell been discharged, but I understand a test made with paraffin for nitrate stains indicated that my nephew had held the gun when it was fired. He's left-handed, and there was a very definite reaction to the paraffin test, so–

called, on his left hand . . . and the sheriff took Dorothy Fenner into custody five hours ago.'

Mason thought that over. 'I was afraid he might do something like that. Did you find the bottle and the letter ?'

'I did not, but the authorities made a rather thorough search of the desk and of the study before admitting me. They may have found it and decided to say nothing for the moment.'

'Look here, if George Alder had fired that gun and the bullet didn't go into his body, where could it have gone ?'

'Apparently nowhere. The only possible place for a bullet to have left that room without leaving a telltale hole was to go through the french doors.

'The medical evidence is that George dropped in his tracks. He fell forward on his face. He was facing the desk when he was shot and his back was to the french doors.'

'How was he dressed ?'

'In slacks and a soft-weave sports coat which he evidently wore quite a bit around the house. He had been painting on his yacht a few days before and there were some paint stains on the coat, and there was also a very small triangular rip on the left coat sleeve near the cuff. If he had been expecting a visitor, and apparently he had, he had not deemed it necessary to dress up. His visitor was one whom he would have greeted informally.'

'Just as one of the family ?' Mason asked.

Dorley Alder smiled dryly. 'I was about to use that same expression, Mr Mason, until I realised that, except for Corrine, who disappeared under such circumstances I have no hopes for her. I am the only member of the family.'

'You have an alibi ?' Mason asked, making his voice light with banter.

Dorley said gravely. 'You are a shrewd lawyer, Mr Mason. Your manner is facetious, but your question is barbed.'

'Well ?' Mason asked.

'I am a bachelor, and a retiring one, Mr Mason. My chief relaxation is reading. I am sixty-three and I had only hoped to continue to draw my annuities from the corporate trust and pursue the even tenor of my ways.

'Both of the other beneficiaries were younger people. I certainly should have been permitted the assumption that the mortality tables would give me a chance to ease out of the picture with the two younger people surviving to inherit the trust funds.

'Now I find myself in a position of sole responsibility and sole beneficiary under the trust fund, and I don't like it. I have no one to whom to leave the money and the responsibilities will probably decrease my life expectancy.

'My alibi is largely circumstantial, such as proof from the man who greased my car yesterday afternoon that the speedometer shows a trip to my nephew's house was out of the question, and evidence that the speedometer had not been disconnected.

'And I am not fool enough, Mr Mason, to think that the authorities are not sceptical and are failing to check my every moment and movement with great care.

'As you can judge, I am very, very busy this morning, Mr Mason. I have a thousand and one things to handle. There is a vast, far-flung empire presided over by our corporation. I confess that I am not fully familiar with the details and I suddenly find myself with a terrific responsibility. Adding to that is the knowledge that there is certainly whispering behind my back. It is not an enviable position.'

Mason nodded.

'But I wanted to drop in to assure you that I meant what I said to you yesterday. You have made a friend and you have an ally, not only individually, but as the surviving member of Alder Associates, Incorporated.'

'Thank you.'

'Among my nephew's things I found one bit of information which I think might be of value to you.'

'What is that?' Mason asked.

'I found that after learning the contents of this letter, my nephew tried frantically to get in touch with Carmen Monterrey.'

'Naturally he would,' Mason said.

'He put ads in the various papers and I have reason to believe that Carmen Monterrey got in touch with him over the telephone. I find on his memo pad a note containing the initials "CM", and an address. The address seems to be that of a Mexican restaurant catering to the tourist trade. I know no more about it than that, but I have brought you the address. I thought that perhaps you might be interested.'

Mason nodded.

'I feel,' Dorley went on, 'that your client's interests will necessitate an investigation of that letter. I think that perhaps you can make that to better advantage than I can, and I am hoping that any information you do secure, you will feel free to communicate to me. I think we will both be in a better and more satisfactory

93

position when the mystery of my nephew's death is cleared up. If it was a suicide let us determine that point. If it was an accidental death due to the unexpected discharge of his gun, let us prove it. And if it was murder, let us apprehend and convict the murderer.

'And I will be willing to contribute time, effort and money to help you in whatever you do along those lines.'

'Thanks. I may call on you.'

'Please do so. If there is some fee . . .'

'Don't misunderstand me on that point,' Mason interrupted. 'Until this is cleared up I have only one client and that's Dorothy Fenner.'

'Yes, yes. I can appreciate your position, Mason. A lawyer can only ride one horse – but after this is all over, I can assure you that I'll then approach you – financially. In the meantime you owe your client everything, and me nothing.

'I deem it fair to tell you that for some strange reason the authorities are rather triumphant over evidence they have found implicating someone, and I *think* that someone is Dorothy Fenner.

'However, you now know my position. Please call on me for any co-operation.'

'Well,' Mason said, 'as you know, I'm representing Dorothy Fenner and I'm also representing this syndicate which has property adjoining yours, and which . . .'

'As far as the syndicate is concerned,' Dorley Alder interrupted, 'you can definitely assure your clients that as soon as the necessary preliminary arrangements have been made so that I can take over the reins, they can count upon the full co-operation of the Alder Associates.'

'You mean you'll join in a fair lease ?' Mason asked.

'Exactly. There has been rather a ruthless policy of exploitation on the part of the corporation,' Dorley Alder explained. 'A policy which I personally have deplored. I want you to feel that so far as lies within my power, and apparently a great deal now does lie within my power, that policy is going to be reversed.'

Mason said, 'That'll be very welcome news. Could you perhaps find time to drop me a note about the oil lease which I could show to my clients in the syndicate ? It would make them feel that I had accomplished something tangible.'

Dorley Alder smiled. 'You are both tactful and shrewd, Mr Mason. I'll send you such a letter within the next few hours by special messenger. In the meantime, here's a memo with the address which I assume is either an address at which Carmen

Monterrey can be reached, or where some definite information about her can be discovered.'

'I want to thank you for your professional courtesies and I can assure you that you will have no reason to regret them. And now, if you'll excuse me, I'm really terribly busy this morning, but I did want you to understand the situation as soon as you came in.'

Alder shook hands and once more made a dignified exit through the door to the corridor without once looking back.

Mason glanced at Della Street, then looked down at the address on the memo pad.

'Well, Della,' he said, 'it looks as though you and I were going to have dinner at a Mexican restaurant tonight.'

'An early dinner?' she asked.

'An early dinner?' Mason said, 'and in the meantime we'll get hold of Paul Drake, give him this address, get him to dig up a description of Carmen Monterrey and put some of his men on the job of watching the place.'

'Sounds like an interesting evening,' Della Street said.

'Darned if it doesn't,' Mason grinned.

'And,' she pointed out, 'if your client was grateful for what you had done up to last night, think of how she's going to feel tonight.'

'I'm afraid to.'

'I think,' Della Street told him, 'you'd better have your secretary take notes during your next interview with Dorothy Fenner. How long will they hold her?'

Mason shrugged his shoulders and said, 'That depends on whether she follows my instructions and doesn't talk.'

'Suppose she doesn't?'

'Then they may hold her for quite a while.'

'Suppose she does talk?'

'Then they'll turn her inside out and let her loose, and promptly start trying to twist her statements so they can be used against her.'

'And what are we going to do?'

'We,' Mason said, smiling, 'are about to prepare an application for writ of habeas corpus, Della, and in the event Dorothy Fenner doesn't communicate with us by two o'clock this afternoon, we'll drive down to call on Judge Lankershim, of Department One, who seems to be a reasonable chap, and get him to issue a writ of habeas corpus. And that will force the sheriff's office to either fish or cut bait.'

'Perhaps they'll decide to fish.'

'Then,' Mason said, grinning, *we'll* cut the bait and try our best to arrange it very temptingly on a very sharp hook.'

CHAPTER TWELVE

Paul Drake said, 'Well, Perry, here's the dope. We've tried our damnedest to trace that woman who was at Los Merritos and find out where she came from. Such a person was there, all right. The description seems to answer that of Corrine Lansing. This person was suffering from amnesia, hallucinations, complete hysteria, and what they refer to as manic-depressive psychosis.

'She was there on the date Minerva Danby wrote that letter. She never did tell them who she was, so they could depend on what she said. She was kept in the south wing where they had that disastrous fire about four months ago. Some half-dozen inmates were burnt alive. She was one of them.'

'The body ?' Mason asked.

'Burnt beyond recognition,' Drake said. 'Identified, however, by means of a metallic tag.'

'Any chance it wasn't the same person ?'

'Lots of chance that it wasn't Corrine Lansing,' Drake said, 'but no chance that it wasn't the person who had been confined there and whom Minerva apparently identified on the day of her death.'

'No other clues ?' Mason asked.

'No. We just can't find out a single thing that will give us a definite answer. She was picked up on the streets of Los Angeles about two o'clock in the morning. The first diagnosis was that she was drunk. She was confined as an alcoholic, then taken to the psychopathic ward, then sent to Los Merritos.'

'That's a private institution ?'

'That's right. Here's what happened. Police naturally were trying to locate relatives. They had this person listed with Missing Persons and all that stuff. A woman who was looking for a sister who had disappeared thought this person answered the description, was taken to see her; said that it was not her sister, but listened to her ravings, became sympathetic and said she would send money for private treatments. The superintendent naturally thought the contribution would be in the form of a cheque. It wasn't. It was in the form of cash, a package of currency which was delivered by messenger, and a note stating that the woman preferred to remain anonymous.'

'In other words,' Mason said, 'there's absolutely no chance of making an identification now, either that the body is or is not that of Corrine Lansing.'

'That's right.'

'Burial ?' Mason asked.

Drake shrugged his shoulders. 'She was listed as *Unidentified Dead*. You know what happens in those cases. The bodies are turned over to the State for purposes of dissection and what have you. They're supposed to be held for thirty days.'

'A burnt body ?' Mason asked.

'I understood they're somewhat in demand, in classes on police administration, arson, criminology, and homicide investigation.'

'And how about this message in the bottle ?'

'If police found it there in Alder's desk they certainly have clammed up. They haven't let out a peep.'

'What do you hear from your client ?'

'I don't. I filed habeas corpus a couple hours ago.'

'The sheriff thinks he has something on her, Perry. Incidentally, police, acting on the sheriff's orders, grabbed the night clerk at the Monadnock Hotel Apartments, and are keeping him sewed up as a material witness. Now why would they want him unless he could give them something on Dorothy ?'

Mason said, 'Damn it, Paul, Dorothy Fenner was in her apartment when the crime was committed. She was released from jail and went directly to her room in the hotel. I drove her up to the place. Now, I'll tell you in confidence why the sheriff wants that night clerk. He *may* be able to prove that George S. Alder came to see Dorothy Fenner at her room at the Monadnock Hotel Apartments, but that's all they can prove. Dorothy Fenner assures me that she was in her room all the time.'

'Well,' Drake said, 'there's something funny about the way they've got this night clerk sewed up, Perry.'

Mason said, 'It's just as I told you, Paul. They've got him sewed up because they want to prove that Alder came to call on Dorothy Fenner. I know all about that. He gave the clerk five dollars to let him go up without being announced. So what ? That doesn't prove anything.'

'Well, the sheriff seems to think it does. They're certainly laying for you.'

'Let them lay,' Mason said grimly. 'They may find they've laid an egg. Did you locate Pete Cadiz ?'

'Yes. He's a specialised sort of beachcomber who lives on a sail-boat. You want us to get a statement ?'

'Gosh, no. Lay off the guy, Paul. I can't even show any interest in him without tipping my hand. I'm not supposed to know anything about that letter. Do you suppose it was taken by the murderer, Paul ?'

'I don't know a thing about it, Perry. All I do know is that the police here are working with the sheriff's office and they're all feeling very smug.'

Mason frowned. 'Hang it, Paul, they *must* be barking up a wrong tree. Have you located Carmen Monterrey ?'

'She's at that restaurant address, acting as hostess and fortune-teller. She'll be there tonight, but no one seems to know where she is today. I have men covering the place. Want anything special on her ?'

Mason shook his head. 'Della and I are going to eat there tonight – and have our fortunes told.'

'Hope you're lucky,' Drake grinned. 'Ask her what the authorities *really* have on your client, Perry. I'm satisfied they *think* they have an ace in the hole.'

'Let 'em have it and we'll trump it,' Mason announced optimistically.

CHAPTER THIRTEEN

A fat Mexican, smiling fixedly in a travesty of carefree good nature, a serape thrown over his shoulders, a big straw sombrero on his head, played a guitar.

He was seated in front of the entrance which went down a short flight of stairs to the basement restaurant and the smile had long since ceased to be anything more than the facial distortion of wearied muscles.

Mason, Della Street on his arm, trying to give the impression of sauntering along, hesitated momentarily in front of the restaurant, then went down the stairs into a dimly lighted dining-room where there was a heavy accent on local colour.

Tables, covered with red-and-white chequered tablecloths,

were grouped around a dance floor which could not have been over fifteen feet square.

At one end was a microphone, and four men with serapes and sombreros furnished music for four or five couples who were dancing. Out of some three dozen tables in the place, about half were filled.

Waitresses in Mexican costume carried food and drinks. A fortune-teller moved about from table to table, smiling impersonally and with a fixed grimace purely as mechanical as that of the lonely guitar player on the outside.

Paul Drake's man moved up to Mason's side, said in a low voice, 'She came in about fifteen minutes ago.'

'She's the fortune-teller?'

'That's right. This is her aunt coming now. The aunt owns the joint.'

The big woman Drake's man had pointed out came sweeping towards them, a smile of welcome on her face, her eyes shrewdly searching.

'Friend of mine,' Drake's operative said. 'I'm over here in the booth. He'll join me.'

'Oh, that ees fine,' the hostess purred. 'Your frien', no?'

'Yes.'

'Oh, that ess so nice. He an' the *senorita* weel be weeth you. I am glad you haf come.'

Mason walked over to the booth indicated by Drake's operative and sat down.

'Had your fortune told?' Mason asked.

'No,' the man said. 'She only came in fifteen minutes ago, and Paul's orders were to case the joint, keep her spotted, find out everything we could about her background, and wait for you.'

'We'll wait a minute and see what's doing.'

Drake's man said, 'The Spanish rice is about the best bet if you're going to eat. The other stuff is pretty heavy. Gosh, when you've once known the real Mexican friendly hospitality, this tourist stuff is ghastly. If you order beer they give you about ten minutes before the waiter comes around, picks up the empty bottle suggestively and gives you the benefit of a silent suggestion to order another one. . . . Watch the dancing, it's good.'

Mason seated himself and watched the couples on the floor.

'The two girls with the older guys are a kick,' the detective said. 'Evidently they're stuck with entertaining some out-of-town buyers. They're not party girls, probably stenographers in the

99

office, and they don't like the job. The men are all organised to go great guns, and are cutting loose and being devilish. The girls would like to have it all over with, and are wondering just what's going to happen when it comes time for good nights. They duck out to the powder-room every twenty minutes or so for a conference, and as soon as they go, the men get their heads together and start plotting in low voices.

'Notice the snaky-looking gal with the tall chap. She has her eye on the situation with the two out-of-town buyers. I'm betting even money that the next time the two girls duck out to the powder-room the snaky gal will do something to attract attention. Notice the way she dances. You'd think she was trying to crawl inside the guy's coat.

'Then notice the guy who's taking his wife out for a celebration. That's more dancing and exercise than he's had in ten years. She's enjoying herself, but they're both going to be stiff in the morning and by tomorrow night at this time the doctor will coil up the stethoscope, shake his head gravely, and tell the fellow he has to remember he's thirty-five years older and forty pounds heavier than he was when he was voted the best dancer in his college class.

'I always like to watch people in a joint like this and . . .'

A waitress handed Perry Mason a menu.

Mason said, 'Bring me some beer and some of those little corn doodads to go with it. Then we'll order.'

The waitress brought beer and *Fritos*, paused for their orders. Mason persuaded Della to try the Spanish rice and *tortillas*.

Della Street said, 'She's coming now, Chief.'

Carmen Monterrey, with a smile, moved over to the table. 'Do you wish your fortunes told?' she asked, arching her eyebrows, glancing at the men but concentrating on Della Street.

'Oh,' Della Street exclaimed enthusiastically, 'that would be . . .' She broke off abruptly and glanced apprehensively at Perry Mason.

Mason, acting the part, said expansively. 'Sure, sure. If you want it, go right ahead.'

Della Street said contritely, 'Oh, I didn't mean – is it all right ?'

'Sure it's all right,' Mason said. He handed Carmen Monterrey three folded dollar notes. 'Here,' he said. 'Give her a good reading.'

Carmen Monterrey slipped the money down the front of her blouse, moved into the vacant seat opposite Della Street, said, 'Let me have your hand.'

For several moments she studied Della Street's hands, then she said, 'You work. You have a very important position. No?'

'That depends on what you mean by important,' Della Street said modestly.

'You love your work,' she said, 'but perhaps that is because you love someone who is connected with the work.'

She raised her eyebrows.

Della Street, Suddenly embarrassed, said, 'Well, after all...'

Carmen Monterrey glanced comprehensively at Perry Mason. 'Oh,' she said, and then added quickly, 'You have such a great loyalty to your work. Perhaps that is because the man you work for is a big man, a noble man. He inspires confidence.'

Mason gravely peeled off another dollar note and handed it to Carmen Monterrey. 'You're doing fine,' he said.

There were dimples on her face as she laughingly added that dollar note to the others.

She said, 'You work very hard, long hours, but you feel that you are a part of this work that you love. And this love will bear fruit – no?'

Della Street started to say something, then checked herself.

'Nice fruit,' Carmen Monterrey said. 'Beautiful fruit. First there comes the blossom, then the fruit... There are times when you wish to rest but you do not wish to leave your work. You have been alone in the world for a long time. Your mother died when you were young and your father... Perhaps there was a separation before your mother died and your mother died from a broken heart – no?

'And this thing has made an impression on you. You have been aware that when a woman gives her heart she gives everything. ... Perhaps...'

Della Street suddenly jerked her hand away.

'That's plenty,' she said, laughing nervously.

Carmen Monterrey looked at her understandingly. 'The future,' she said, 'is perhaps even now shaped by the past. The ship that never leaves port because it is afraid of the storms cannot bring back a wealthy cargo – no?'

'No,' Della Street agreed.

Carmen Monterrey glanced at Perry Mason, started to reach for his hand, but turned instead to Harry Frink. 'Do you wish your fortune told – no?'

'No,' Frink said, shortly and emphatically.

Mason said, 'I think you're a pretty good fortune-teller, Miss...'

'Carmen,' she said, 'call me Carmen.'

'You're good.'

'I have always been psychic. I can see things. And sometimes in the lines of the hand . . .'

'Do you really believe that ?' Mason asked.

She shrugged and laughed. 'How do I know what I believe ? When one believes something it is a part of one. I only know that when I take the hand of a person I feel something come to me. It flows from that hand into mine, then into my blood and into my brain, and ideas come. I look at the lines on the hand and I hold the hand, but the things form in my brain. That is what you call psychic – no ?'

'I suppose so,' Mason said dubiously. 'Were you born here ?' She shook her head. 'I was born in Mexico.'

'You are wise,' Mason said. 'You have travelled – no ?'

She laughed and said, 'Already you have acquired the Mexican custom of ending a sentence with a question. My aunt laughs at me about that habit but she has it herself. We will make a question and say "no" on the end when perhaps the answer, of course, is "yes" but we say "no" as a question to make it easy for the person who answers.'

'Where were you educated ?' Mason asked.

'I have travelled,' she said, somewhat wistfully.

'Europe ?'

'No.'

'South America ?'

She nodded.

Mason said, 'I have always wanted to go to South America. Tell me, is it beautiful ?'

Carmen rolled her eyes. 'Oh, *Senor*, it is beeeeeautiful.'

'It is long since you have been there ?'

'I have but just returned.'

'Indeed.'

'This thing which enables me to tell fortunes, works for others, but in my own case I cannot see things so clear. My one great friend, she disappeared and no one knows where she has gone. Some say she must be dead. But they cannot say when she died or how she died. For myself I can only admit I do not know.

'Sometimes I feel she is alive and very close, but sometimes I feel she is dead and very close. It is a puzzle. She had trouble with her mind before she died, and when a friend whom she trusted betrayed her confidence it was a great shock.

102

'But we talk about me too much. It is better to talk about you. You have many talents, you have things for which others may well envy you, but you are in great danger – no?'

'No,' Mason said, smiling.

'Oh, but I think you are. I think even now there are . . . but you perhaps do not wish to have your fortune told – no?'

Mason threw back his head and laughed. 'Your salesmanship is charming. Certainly I wish my fortune told.'

She took his hand, held it for moment.

Suddenly Frink coughed warningly, caught Mason's eye and gestured.

Mason looked up to see two men, broad-shouldered, wary in their bearing, yet aggressively important, enter the restaurant.

The Mexican woman who ran the place came to them cordially, then, as she saw the unmistakable stamp of official importance on their faces, the smile froze on her lips.

One of the men said something in a low voice.

The woman pointed towards the booth.

The two men walked over, one of them pulled back his coat, showed his star. 'All right, Carmen,' he said, 'that's enough. Get your things on. You're coming with us. Someone wants to ask you questions.'

He looked impersonally at Mason, said, 'Sorry to interrupt your party, mister,' and put his hand on Carmen's shoulder.

'Let's get going, Carmen,' he said.

'But I do not understand . . .'

'Never mind, come on.'

The woman who ran the place was solicitous. 'Please, Carmen, queek,' she said, and then broke into a rattle of Spanish, which galvanised Carmen into action.

'Well,' Mason said as the men escorted Carmen to a car, 'it was good while it lasted. I'll call Paul Drake and see if he knows about this angle.'

He went to the phone booth, dialled Drake's number and when he had the detective on the line said, 'They just picked Carmen up, Paul. Know anything about it?'

'I don't *know*, Perry, but I *think* the authorities have that letter in the bottle and they're intending to launch an investigation. However, I have some other news. Did Carmen tell your fortune?'

'Yes.'

'How was it?'

'She's good, Paul – a natural psychic.'

'Was it a good fortune?'

'What there was of it. She was interrupted.'

'If it was good,' Drake said, 'she's a rotten psychic. The word has just been passed that the sheriff has a dead-open-and-shut case against Dorothy Fenner and that he's prepared to prove *you* were the accomplice who waited for her in the canoe when she tried to steal evidence from George Alder's house Saturday night.'

CHAPTER FOURTEEN

'The peremptory challenge is with the defendant,' Judge Garey said.

Perry Mason, on his feet, bowed urbanely. 'We are thoroughly satisfied with this jury, Your Honour.'

Judge Garey glanced at the prosecutor.

Claud Gloster, district attorney, made a gesture, a sweeping inclusive gesture of approval. 'Swear the jury.'

Judge Garey said, 'The clerk will swear the jury.'

The jury of seven men and five women rose, held up their right hands and were sworn to try the issues well and faithfully in the case of the People of the State of California on the one hand and Dorothy Fenner on the other.

Claud Gloster, as prosecutor, made a very brief opening statement in which he stated merely that he expected to prove the defendant, Dorothy Fenner, with malice aforethought, had murdered George S. Alder at his house at the beach on a place known as Alder Island; that death had been caused by gunshot; that the bullet had penetrated the neck, severed a main artery and shattered the spine. The victim had dropped in his tracks.

The victim had been expecting the defendant to call on him. He had locked up the dog which had been his inseparable companion for the past few months so that the defendant could come to the house without fear of the dog. The defendant had killed him with one shot from a .38-calibre revolver, fled out of the back door to the beach where she had left a canoe or some small boat, had rowed out to her own yacht, tied the boat to the yacht, changed her clothes, gone to the landing pier, and returned to her apartment.

It was a very sketchy opening speech. At the end of it, the prosecutor sat down. Mason waived his opening speech at that time and the district attorney called his first witness.

The autopsy surgeon testified with a bristling of technical language to the fact of death and the cause of death.

Claud Gloster, a careful, logical, dangerous court-room antagonist, was careful to ask just the right questions to bring out the points he wanted and then stop.

'Do you,' he asked, turning to Mason courteously, 'wish to cross-examine the witness, Mr Mason?'

'Just a question,' Mason said.

'Go right ahead.'

'Thank you. Doctor, when you examined the body, you determined the cause of death?'

'Yes, sir.'

'You have mentioned that the wound was caused by a .38-calibre bullet?'

'Yes, sir.'

'That bullet was recovered then?'

'No, sir, the bullet was not recovered.'

'How, then, do you know the calibre?'

'From the size of the wound in part, in part by deduction from the fact that the gun which fired the fatal bullet was lying under the body.'

'If you didn't find the fatal bullet, how do you know this gun which was found under the body was the weapon which fired the fatal bullet?'

'Because it had been recently discharged, because there was no other place where the bullet could have gone, and because the gun was a .38-calibre.'

'I see. You know the fatal bullet was a .38-calibre because the gun was found beneath the body, and you know this weapon was the weapon used because it's a .38-calibre. Is that right?'

'It makes it sound absurd when you express it that way.'

'Then express your deductions in some way so they won't sound absurd.'

'There was the size of the wound.'

'Don't you know a bullet always makes a smaller entrance wound than the calibre of the bullet?'

'How can it make an entrance wound that is *smaller* than its diameter?'

'Due to the elasticity of the skin.'

'Well, this was a .38-calibre. I'm certain of it.'

'But that part of your testimony about the gun being the fatal gun is pure deduction?'

'It's a matter of expert opinion.'

'An expert opinion based on pure deduction, Doctor?'

'Well – yes, if you want to put it that way.'

'That's all' Mason said.

A surveyor was sworn and maps of the premises were introduced. Then a police officer who testified that he was called to the scene of the crime because of a telephone call from a neighbour who had in turn been alarmed by the screams of one of the servants who had been to a movie and returned to find George Alder lying dead on the floor of the study. The officer described the premises as he had found them, stated that from the time he entered the premises he remained on duty, that he instructed others to telephone the sheriff and notify the coroner. The witness waited on the premises until the coroner arrived. He was present when photographs were taken and he identified a long series of photographs showing the body of the dead man and the condition of the premises at that time.'

'Cross-examine' Gloster said, quite casually.

'Now, the dog was shut up in an adjoining room?' Mason asked.

'It wasn't an adjoining room, it was sort of a – well, a closet with a ventilator in it and a window up near the top. The window was so high that the dog couldn't reach it.'

'Who let the dog out?'

'Well, after reinforcements came we – we all sort of let him out together.'

'And what happened?'

The officer said, 'We tried to open the door a crack and then as he pushed his head out, slip a rope around his neck.'

'Were you able to do so?'

The officer grinned. 'That dog was just like a bullet. We opened that door and the dog came out of there like a shot, jerked the rope out of the hands of the man who was trying to hold him, and went out of there like greased lightning.'

'Where did he go?'

'The last I saw of him he was crossing the room and tearing down the side stairs, the rope whipping behind him.'

'You ran out after him?'

'Yes, sir.'

'And where was he?'

The witness grinned. 'He was gone.'

That sally brought laughter from the court-room.

'Do you know in which direction the dog went?'

'Well, not from my personal knowledge, no, sir.'

'He wasn't visible in the yard?'

'No, sir.'

'You do know that he was not in the back yard?'

'He ran around the side of the house apparently, and tried to get out to the street through the gate. I don't *know* this, I can't swear to it because by the time I got around to the front of the house the servant who had run out of the front door had the rope and was holding him.'

'Did the dog make any attempt to bite?'

'The dog let this servant hold the rope.'

'That was the same servant who had discovered the body?'

'Yes, sir.'

'And where is that dog now?'

'Oh, Your Honour,' Gloster said, 'that's certainly not proper cross-examination. It's far outside of the issues.'

'Well, if the witness knows, he may tell,' the judge ruled. 'I don't see that it's particularly important one way or the other, but I want to give counsel the greatest latitude in cross-examination.'

'But, Your Honour, the question of where the dog is at the *present* time is certainly carrying an inquiry far afield' Gloster said courteously. 'I think that it is significant that the deceased locked the dog up in this closet so that the visitor whom he was expecting would not be annoyed by the dog. We expect to prove that that was somewhat a routine procedure. Whenever anyone was admitted to the house – any stranger, that is, the dog was either shut up or kept on leash. But where the dog is now, that's going far outside the issues.'

Mason said with a smile, 'Well, if it's entirely immaterial why not let me know where the dog is?'

'Because there's no use cluttering up the record with a lot of extraneous matters.'

'Well, just for my own information, tell me where the dog is.' Gloster shook his head.

Judge Garey began to show signs of quick interest. 'I think the defence is entitled to know,' he ruled.

'Your Honour,' Gloster said desperately, 'I want to keep the evidence within the issues and I want to keep the issues narrowed down to the question of who killed George S. Alder. If we get to bringing dogs into the case, and where the dogs are, and what the dogs are eating, and how the dogs feel, and whether the dogs are mourning, and . . .'

'He hasn't asked anything about the dog's diet. He's asking where the dog is,' Judge Garey said, 'and I think he's entitled to know. Answer the question, Mr Witness.'

'I don't know,' the officer said. 'He was, I believe, taken out to some boarding kennel. That's the last I heard of it.'

'Do you know the name of the kennel, Mr Gloster?' Judge Garey asked, his voice ominous.

'No, Your Honour, I believe the sheriff had charge of the dog.'

'Well, find out and let me know,' Judge Garey said. 'I think we're entitled to know where the dog is. Any further cross-examination, Mr Mason?'

'This closet that the dog was in,' Mason said. 'Did you say the closet had been specially built for the dog?'

'No, sir, I didn't. I think it had just been a closet that had had a ventilator put in it. You could see the dog had been kept in there at intervals – there was a bed, a pan of water, and the inside of the door was just scratched all to pieces where the dog had tried to get out when the murder was committed. He had torn a nail loose in his clawing.'

'You noticed the torn claw?' Mason asked.

'Not the torn claw, but you could see that it had been torn because there were three distinct, although faint, streaks of blood on the inside of the door where his paw had scratched along the wood, and a couple of bloody smudges on the closet floor. If you ask me, it was a crime to leave a dog in a room with a panelled door like that. A smooth piece of wood could have been fastened to the inside of the door and then the dog wouldn't have torn his nails on the panels.'

'But had he scratched on the door before?' Mason asked.

'Well, to be fair to the owner, the scratches were all fresh. I presume that . . . I'm sorry, I forgot I can't testify to an opinion.'

'Go right ahead,' Mason told him. 'I'm not objecting. You seem to have a more expert opinion than the experts.'

The witness grinned. 'Well, the scratches on the inside of the door were all fresh. I called the attention of the others to that after we'd opened the door and the dog had dashed out. Evidently he'd been well disciplined and accustomed to remaining in the closet, but when he heard the shot fired and – well, I presume there'd been a quarrel and – well, anyway, that dog wanted to get out so bad he'd torn a nail on that rough panelling on the inside of the door. I'm a dog lover and it makes me sore when I see an animal abused.'

'More than one claw torn loose ?' Mason asked.

'I'd say just one.'

'And no scratches on the door that weren't fresh ?'

'No, sir. Incidentally, I verified that from the servants, but I presume that wouldn't be admissible as evidence now.'

'In other words,' Mason said, 'you were trying to prove at least to your own satisfaction that there'd been something of a quarrel immediately preceding the shooting. Is that right ?'

'Yes, sir.'

'And you did so ?'

'Exactly.'

'Then, since we're dealing in theories, how did the murderer get possession of George Alder's gun ?'

'It must have been lying on the desk . . . or, perhaps a young woman . . .'

'Oh, if the Court *please*,' Claud Gloster protested.

'All this certainly isn't evidence,' Judge Garey ruled. 'It's pure speculation. Counsel is asking for it, but it's not evidence.'

'It's just like all the rest of the case, Your Honour,' Mason said.

'I think we'll dispense with discussion, Mr Mason.'

'Very well, Your Honour.'

'That's all,' Gloster announced. 'Now my next witness will be the sheriff of the county, Leonard C. Keddie.'

Sheriff Keddie, a tall, rawboned, slow-speaking individual, duly sworn, settled himself on the witness-stand and gave his name, age, and occupation.

'You were called to the residence of George S. Alder on Alder Island on the night of August third ?'

'I was, yes, sir.'

'And what did you find, Sheriff ?'

'Well, when I arrived there the others had already been there – they'd been there some little time. I organised the search, and started looking around. We found that a boat was missing from the landing – one of the small boats, and assumed that the murderer might have managed to escape in that. There was a burglar alarm on the wharf, but a person who knew the layout could switch that alarm off *from the land side*, so that it would be inoperative for about three minutes and then would go on again.

I took charge of the phase of the investigation which had for its object the finding of that boat.'

'And did you find it ?'

'Yes, sir.'

'Where ?'

'Drifting in the bay.'

'Can you point on this map, People's Exhibit D-twelve, to show approximately where the boat was recovered ?'

'Yes sir, I can. It was right about at this point where I will now make a cross in pencil.'

'Now, were you present when that boat was recovered ?'

'Yes, sir.'

'And did you notice anything peculiar about that boat ?'

'It had been freshly painted, a certain green colour.'

'Did you make any investigation of the yacht, the *Kathy-Kay*, owned by the defendant in this case ?'

'Yes, sir.'

'And did you notice anything significant on that yacht ?'

'Yes, sir.'

'What ?'

'A place where some green paint had been rubbed against the side of the yacht.'

'And what did you do with that green paint, if anything ?'

'I saw that it was removed and taken to a chemical laboratory for a spectroscopic analysis in comparison with the paint on this light boat which we found drifting in the bay, and which we subsequently identified as having been the property of George S. Alder.'

'What else did you do ?' Gloster asked.

'Well, the sheriff drawled, 'thinking that someone who'd jumped in that boat in a hurry might have dropped something – just on the off chance I got a waterglass and started looking around the bottom of the bay about where the little skiff had been tied up.'

'And did you find anything ?' Gloster asked, glancing triumphantly.

'Yes, sir.'

'What ?'

'A woman's purse.'

'And where is that purse now ?'

'I have it with me,' the sheriff said.

'Will you produce it, please ?'

The sheriff opened a bag and produced a heavy Manila envelope encrusted with red sealing wax and signatures.

'It's right here, all sealed up in this envelope.'

'Now, did you make an inventory of the contents of this purse?'

'I did, yes, sir.'

'And where are the articles which were contained in the purse?'

'I have them here, sir, in this second envelope.'

The witness produced another sealed envelope.

'Now, those envelopes appear to be sealed and to have various signatures on them?'

'Yes, sir.'

'What are those signatures?'

'I signed my name on the envelope when the purse was sealed inside the envelope. The other officers who were there did likewise.'

'And the contents of the purse?'

'Those were placed in another envelope and these signatures are the signatures of the other witnesses.'

'And your signature is on both envelopes?'

'It is, yes, sir.'

'And are you satisfied that the seals have not been tampered with?'

'Yes, sir.'

'I believe my signature is also on there,' Claud Gloster said, smilingly.

'Yes, sir.'

'I'll take a look at that, and I'll ask that the envelopes be passed to the jurors so that each juror can observe that the seals have not been tampered with.'

'Any objection?' Judge Garey asked Mason.

'None whatever, Your Honour.'

The envelopes were passed around for the inspection of the jury, then the district attorney said, 'I now ask that these envelopes be opened and the various articles be received in evidence. The purse as one exhibit, and the envelope containing the contents as another exhibit.'

Mason said, 'I would like to interpose an objection, Your Honour, and would like the privilege of cross-examining the witness concerning the two exhibits in connection with my objection.'

'Very well.'

Mason faced the sheriff and said, 'By using a waterglass, you saw this woman's purse lying on the bottom of the bay?'

'Yes, sir, aided by the beam of a flashlight.'

'Sand or muddy bottom?'

'Sandy at that point. A white sand. The purse showed up very plainly.'

'Exactly,' Mason said. 'And that purse was lying where you could see it with a waterglass while you were lying face down on the little landing wharf?'

'Yes, sir.'

'The purse was then very close to the wharf?'

'Yes, sir.'

'Where anyone could have dropped it while standing on the wharf?'

'Where a woman would most naturally have dropped it in jumping from the wharf to a boat.'

Mason said, 'Just answer my question, if you will, please, Sheriff. The purse was lying on the bottom where it could have been dropped by a person standing on the wharf?'

'Well, I suppose so, yes, but in that event a woman would certainly know she had dropped the purse and . . .'

'Exactly,' Mason interrupted. 'I see that you're quite anxious to make your point, Sheriff, so we'll concede it. But the fact remains that the purse *could* quite readily have been dropped by someone standing on the wharf.'

'Well, it could have been, yes.'

'Now, you saw this purse lying on the bottom, and then what did you do?'

'I recovered it.'

'How?'

'By going in after it.'

'How deep was the water?'

'Oh, I would say six or seven feet.'

'And who went in after it?'

'One of my deputies.'

'Oh,' Mason said, smiling, 'you discovered the purse and then sent one of your deputies in after it.'

'I have a deputy who's a very good swimmer.'

'And he brought the purse out?'

'Yes.'

'Now, Sheriff, there was nothing about that purse itself that showed you *when* it had been dropped?'

'Well, when you come right down to it, if you take a look at the . . .'

112

Mason interrupted firmly, 'Sheriff, I'm going to insist on a categorical answer to my question. There was nothing about that purse which indicated *when* it had been dropped. I'm speaking now about the purse itself.'

'No, sir.'

'It was simply lying there on the sand.'

'Well, of course, it couldn't have stayed right there in that position on the sand very long.'

'Why not, Sheriff?'

'Well, there's the question of tides and sand drifting in.'

'How long would it have stayed there without having been covered with sand? Remember now, you're on oath, Sheriff.'

'Well . . . of course I don't know.'

'I gathered that you didn't,' Mason said, smiling. 'Now, since you have stated quite frankly there was nothing about the purse which would show *when* it was dropped, for all you know that purse could have been dropped by anyone, including the defendant, the Saturday night before the murder.'

'You're talking about the purse now?'

'About the purse,' Mason said.

'Well, if you want to limit it to the purse, I guess so, but when you take the contents . . .'

'I'm talking now about the purse,' Mason said.

'Very well, about the purse.'

'There was nothing that would indicate the purse couldn't have been dropped on Saturday night?'

'Well, I guess not, no, sir.'

'Now, did you know anything about the defendant having been out at that place the Saturday night before the murder?'

'No, sir, not of my own knowledge.'

'Well, do you know anything at all about it?'

'Oh, Your Honour,' Gloster said, 'I'm going to object to anything that the sheriff doesn't know of his own knowledge.'

'That's quite right,' Mason said. 'I thought perhaps you were going to bring the facts out sooner or later and we might as well get them before the Court.'

Gloster said, 'The only facts I intend to bring out are the facts indicating that this defendant murdered George Alder. If there are any other facts it's up to the defence to bring them out.'

Mason gave that matter frowning consideration for a moment, then said, 'Very well, if that's your position I'll remain within the technical limitations of evidence and expect you to do the same, sir.'

The sheriff volunteered a statement. 'The contents of the purse show when it was dropped,' he said.

'The contents?' Mason asked.

'When we looked inside the purse,' the sheriff explained, grinning triumphantly, 'we found a clipping which had been cut from the *Express* on the morning of the third, a clipping which related to a fifty thousand dollar jewel burglary, and the complaint of Alder that . . .'

'Just a moment, Sheriff,' Mason said. 'The clipping itself is the best evidence, not your recollection of its contents.'

'Very well. The clipping's right here.'

Mason hesitated for a moment while he gave the situation swift consideration, then he said, 'Now, Your Honour, I am going to object to the introduction of the purse itself on the grounds that no proper foundation has been laid as to a question of time, and I am going to object to the contents of the purse being received in evidence on the ground that the contents are incompetent, irrelevant and immaterial, except insofar as those contents may show the ownership of the purse. I am going to object particularly to any newspaper clipping by which the prosecution may seek to prejudice the defendant in the eyes of the jury.'

'Of course, Your Honour,' Gloster pointed out, 'if the contents of the purse are material and relevant, and we insist they are, the fact that they may also disclose matters which the defence would like to keep from this jury does not affect their being received in evidence.'

'Let me take a look at the contents of that purse,' Judge Garey said.

The sheriff handed up the envelope.

Judge Garey inserted his hand in the envelope, fumbled through the contents for a moment, then dumped them all on his desk, made a painstaking inventory, and he seemed considerably interested in the newspaper clipping.

'This clipping was from the *Express*?' he asked.

'On the morning of the third,' Gloster said.

'Under those circumstances, it would seem to be relevant. Of course, the Court will permit its introduction in evidence solely for the purpose of proving the date at which the purse must have been dropped into the water. It will not be evidence as to anything contained in the clipping itself. That is, any matters set forth in the clipping are not part of the evidence in this case, and the jury will be instructed to limit their consideration to the question of time.'

Mason said, 'Your Honour, you'll recognise that in view of the contents of that clipping it would be absolutely impossible for any human being on the jury to follow the Court's instructions and limit the consideration they are to give it.'

'Well,' Judge Garey said, 'the Court gives the instructions. The rest of it is up to the conscience of the jurors.'

Mason said. 'If we are going to open the door, I would much prefer to have all of the evidence brought in and treat the entire transaction as part of the *res gestae*. Let's have the court record as to what happened in connection with the charge made.'

'I don't want it handled that way,' Gloster said. 'I'll put on the prosecution's case and if the defendant wants to put in any justi-fication or any other matters that's the defendant's privilege . . . providing only the evidence is pertinent. But the thing he's asking for now won't be pertinent. We're trying a murder case, not a burglary which took place some time previously. All we want to show by this clipping *when* the purse was dropped into the water.'

'All right, then,' Mason said, 'I'll stipulate that the testimony will be that the purse contained a clipping which came from a newspaper published on the day of the murder, and with that stipulation the prosecution won't need to put the clipping into evidence.'

'I don't want your stipulation,' Gloster said. 'I want the jury to judge that clipping.'

'You see, Your Honour,' Mason said. 'He wants to have the jurors read the clipping and be prejudiced by the contents. This talk of limiting the purpose for which it is to be introduced is utterly meaningless.'

Judge Garey said, 'The question of the date is rather important there, and if this newspaper clipping is from a paper which didn't appear on the streets till around noon on the third, and the purse was recovered on the evening of the third shortly after the murder had been committed, the Court would seem to have no alternative but to admit this as evidence but limit it purely for the purpose of showing date . . . unless Counsel wishes to accept your stipulation, and apparently Counsel does not.'

Mason said, 'Very well, Your Honour, I have two or three additional questions to ask about the purse itself.'

'Go ahead.'

'Now, Sheriff, you have stated that when this purse was recovered it was placed in an envelope and sealed. The contents were placed in another envelope and that envelope was sealed.'

'Yes, sir.'

'And the various parties present wrote their names on the envelopes?'

'That's right.'

'And the envelopes were then sealed?'

'Yes, sir.'

'*When* was this done?'

'Almost immediately after the purse was recovered.'

'What do you mean by almost immediately?'

'Well, within a very short time.'

'What do you mean by a short time?'

'I can't express it any better than that.'

'As much as an hour?'

'I would say almost immediately, Mr Mason. I can't time it in a question of minutes.'

'No,' Mason said, 'you would prefer to leave it in terms of generality, wouldn't you, Sheriff?'

'What do you mean by that?'

'You don't *dare* to tie it down to any particular period of time.'

The sheriff flushed and said, 'That's not the case, Mr Mason. I had a great many things on my mind that night, and all I can say is that it was done almost immediately after the purse was recovered. I wasn't wearing a stop-watch.'

Gloster permitted himself an audible chuckle and glanced at the jury to see if they approved. An answering smile or two convinced him he had done right, and had the approval of the jury.

Mason said, 'I notice some of these signatures are in pencil and some are in ink, Sheriff.'

'That's right. Mine is in ink. Some of them are in pencil.'

'All made at the same time?'

'All made at the same time.'

'Almost immediately after the purse was recovered?'

'Almost immediately after the purse was recovered.'

'Now, then,' Mason said, 'can you tell me how these signatures were made?'

'How does anyone make his signature? He writes his name,' the sheriff said irritably.

'Oh, Your Honour,' Gloster said, 'this examination is going far afield. Counsel is evidently sparring for time.'

Judge Garey said, 'It would seem to me, Mr Mason, that you have already explored the possibilities of the situation.'

'If your honour will bear with me,' Mason said, 'I am about to make a point which I think will be of great importance.'

'Very well, go ahead.'

Mason took the envelope, placed the purse in the envelope, then held a sheet of paper over the envelope. 'Now, go ahead and sign your name,' he said to the sheriff.

'What's the idea?'

'I simply want to compare your figures.'

The sheriff took a fountain-pen from his pocket, balanced the envelope on his knees, and started to write his name on the piece of paper, then frowned, pushed the envelope to one side and placed the paper on the judge's desk.

'No, no,' Mason said. 'Hold the paper right over the purse.'

The sheriff wrote his name.

Mason took the paper, said, 'Thank you, Sheriff,' produced another sheet of paper which he placed on the judge's desk, and said, 'Now please sign your name once more on *this* sheet of paper.'

'I don't see why,' the sheriff growled.

'Simply to compare the signatures,' Mason said.

The sheriff, with poor grace, signed his name and resumed his position on the witness-stand.

'Exactly as I thought,' Mason said.

'What is?' the sheriff demanded irritably.

'You can see,' Mason said, 'by comparing the signatures, that this signature which you made when the purse was in the envelope is certainly not the same as the signature which is on the envelope.'

'Well, that purse got in the way. You can't write your name over an object that bulges all over the place.'

'Exactly,' Mason said. 'It's a physical impossibility to sign your name under such circumstances so that the signature compares with a signature such as is on this piece of paper which you made on the judge's desk.'

'Well, then, why did you have me do it?' the sheriff asked.

'Because,' Mason said triumphantly, pointing to the sheriff's signature on the envelope, 'you can see that your signature on the envelope, and the signatures of all these other gentlemen on the envelope are perfect signatures. They *couldn't* have been made while the purse was in the envelope. Moreover, Sheriff, I'll call your attention to the fact that when the purse was taken out of the water it must have been soaking wet. It couldn't have been put in this envelope in that condition without soaking the paper in the envelope so that any ink would have run all over the envelope when a fountain-pen was placed on it. Now, then, can you explain these perfect signatures to the Court and the jury?'

'Well, sure,' the sheriff said. 'We couldn't sign our names with the purse in the envelope. We simply all signed our names on the envelope before we put the purse in. That's the only way our signatures would have meant anything.'

'Oh, then,' Mason said, 'you, and the gentlemen with you, signed an empty envelope. Is that it?'

'I didn't say that. I said we signed the envelope *before* the purse was put in it.'

'How long before?'

'Immediately before.'

'What do you mean by immediately? A matter of seconds, a matter of hours, or a matter of days?'

'I told you I didn't carry a stop-watch with me.'

'But the fact remains,' Mason said, 'that you did sign an *empty* envelope.'

The sheriff, half-raising himself from the chair, shouted, 'I told you we signed it just before the purse was put in it.'

'All right,' Mason said. 'Much as you dislike to admit it, you all signed an empty envelope. Now, then, how does it happen that when that purse was put in it, if it was dripping wet, the water didn't blur the fresh ink on the signatures, and didn't soak the paper of this envelope so that even after drying the marks of moisture would still remain on the envelope?'

'I . . . well, as to that . . .' the sheriff said.

He glanced uncomfortably at Gloster, crossed his legs, uncrossed them, shifted his position, and stroked the angle of his jaw.

'I'm waiting for an answer,' Mason said.

'Well, of course,' the sheriff said, 'you couldn't put a soaking wet purse into a paper envelope. That's absurd.'

'Well, what did you do?'

'Well, I put the purse in the envelope and sealed it.'

'When?'

'Well, within a reasonable time after it had been recovered.'

'Oh,' Mason said, 'now it's a reasonable time. Before it was immediately after. A matter of seconds, I believe you said.'

'Well, I didn't carry a stop-watch.'

'You keep saying that, Sheriff, but the physical appearance of the envelope would indicate that the purse was entirely dry before it was placed in the envelope. Now, suppose you tell us exactly what happened.'

'Well,' the sheriff blurted, 'when I recovered the purse I told the fellows that were with me that we'd have to identify it some way, and I told them we could all sign an envelope and I'd seal it. I had these envelopes with me and we signed them, but – well, naturally, I couldn't put the wet purse in there. I waited until the purse dried.'

'How long?'

'Well, I don't know. I don't know how to answer that question. I was given the responsibility of seeing that purse was put in that signed envelope. I put it there personally. These gentlemen left it to me to do that, and I did it. I accepted that responsibility.'

'After waiting for how long, Sheriff?'

'I simply waited for the purse to dry.'

'So all that the signatures on this envelope mean is that the men who were with you, at your suggestion, signed an empty envelope on the theory that they could in that way identify the purse when it was introduced in evidence, and left it to you to put the purse in the envelope, at a later date.'

'Not at a later *date*, at a later *time*.'

'You don't remember when it was?' Mason asked.

'Not the exact hour, no.'

'Do you remember the exact day?'

The sheriff again shifted his position and said, 'I've already answered that.'

'And we'll now consider the envelope containing the contents of the purse,' Mason said. 'Apparently there are keys, cards, a compact, a cigarette lighter – and yet the signatures on the envelope are perfect signatures. I presume the same holds true as to the signatures on this envelope.'

'Yes, sir.'

'In other words, the men, at your suggestion, signed the empty envelope and you inserted the contents at a much later date.'

'Not at a much later date, pretty soon afterwards.'

'You yourself have said that the purse and the contents were placed in the different envelopes at the same time, and you have

119

stated that the purse was placed in the envelope after it had been thoroughly dried.'

'Well, the stuff was in my possession all the time. Nothing happened to it,' the sheriff said.

'Where did you leave the purse?'

'In my office.'

'And you didn't stay in your office till the purse dried?'

'Well, I put it in front of an electric heater so it would dry out more rapidly.'

'And how long did it take to dry out?'

'I tell you I don't know.'

'But it may have been a day or two later when you put this purse in the envelope.'

'If you're going to be technical about it, I don't know.'

'Thank you,' Mason said, smiling. 'I'm going to be technical about it.'

'And now, Your Honour,' Mason said, turning to Judge Garey, 'it appears that the whereabouts of this purse cannot adequately be explained, and that it is quite possible that the clipping could have been inserted among the contents of this envelope at any time during a two-day period while the purse was drying out. The Court will notice that there is no appreciable evidence of salt water on the clipping.'

'The clipping was inside of a little case,' the sheriff said. 'Sort of a compact arrangement.'

Judge Garey frowned thoughtfully, said, 'I don't think there has been any attempt to mislead the Court, but it certainly must be apparent to the sheriff that having all of these signatures on this envelope is exceedingly misleading. It now appears the parties signed an empty envelope and then gave it into the custody of the sheriff with the understanding that the evidence would be placed in it. The Court is not prepared to rule on the admissibility of the purse at the present time, but will take the matter under advisement.

'It is approaching the hour for adjournment, Mr District Attorney, and . . .'

'I have just a few more questions of this witness.'

'Very well.'

Gloster's manner had lost its triumphant assurance. He was on the defensive now and unquestionably angry about it.

'What else did you do when you went aboard the defendant's boat that night, Sheriff?'

'I looked the place over.'

'What did you find?'

'I found a skirt that was soaking wet with salt water, and on the front of that skirt at a position where the right knee would be, in case a person wearing the skirt knelt over, I found a spot which still contained a little pinkish colour.'

'What did you do with that?'

'I turned that over to a laboratory technician to determine whether or not it was blood.'

'Now, then, Your Honour,' Gloster said, smiling, 'I'm *quite* willing to have a recess taken.'

'Very well,' Judge Garey said. 'The Court will adjourn until ten o'clock tomorrow morning.'

CHAPTER FIFTEEN

Dorothy Fenner looked anxiously around for the matron. 'I'll see you in the morning,' she said.

'Just a minute,' Mason told her. 'I want to ask you a question . . . Dorothy, look at me . . . Dorothy, turn around and look up here.'

She hesitated a moment, then her lips began to twitch.

'No, no,' Mason said, 'you little fool. Don't start crying. People are looking at you. Tell me, did you go down there? *Did* you . . .'

She lowered her eyes.

Mason said, 'Let's pretend that we're talking about some casual matter. Here.' He took a letter from his briefcase, thrust it in front of her, and said, 'Pretend to be reading this. Now tell me, did you go down there?'

'I . . . I . . .'

Mason said, 'If you start bawling now, with newspaper people and spectators watching you, you're signing a one-way ticket to the death cell. Now tell me the truth. *Did* you go down there?'

'Yes,' she said, almost in a whisper.

'Keep talking.'

She said, 'He was going to make a settlement. He made it sound so convincing . . . I went down there just like he told me to. I found the gate open just as he said it would be. I walked in, went around to the side entrance, entered the study and found him lying there on the floor in a big pool of blood. I ran over to him and spoke to him. He didn't answer. I knelt down and felt his skin and then I knew he was dead. And just about that time I heard someone scream behind me.

'I had enough presence of mind not to look around, so that person never did see my face. I simply dashed out through the french doors and out towards the landing wharf.

'Then I knew I was trapped on the island. I could hear this woman behind me running, screaming back across the bridge to the mainland. I only had a matter of minutes and I worked fast. I remembered there was a current interrupter which would shut off the burglar alarm at the landing float for about three minutes, in case Mr Alder wanted to go out in one of the speedboats. So I pushed this current interrupter, ran out on the pier, and found a small boat tied up by a painter. I jumped in and cast loose the painter. When I jumped in I must have dropped my purse but I was too excited to realise it or know anything about it at the time.'

'I knew there was a big spot of blood on my skirt and it had soaked through to the stocking.

'I rowed out into the bay, then just before I got to my yacht I stood up and slipped the skirt off and scrubbed the spot out of it as best I could. Then I boarded my yacht, hurriedly changed into dungarees, jumped into the boat, rowed ashore, shipped the oars and kicked the boat loose. Then I walked to the bus terminal and got aboard a bus. It wasn't until I got started to town that I realised that I'd lost my purse. However, I always carry a spare key to my apartment and a dollar note in the top of my stocking. That's mad money. So I managed to get home all right.'

'Anyone see you come in?' Mason asked.

She said, 'I was frightened. I went around through the back entrance down to the trunk-room and went up to my apartment that way. There's not a soul in the world can prove that I wasn't in that apartment.'

Mason said angrily, 'In addition to being a poor liar, you're a little fool. Why did you lie to me?'

'Honestly, Mr Mason,' she said, 'I feel terribly about this. I wouldn't let you down for anything in the world. Well, I felt absolutely certain I could get away with it and that no one would ever know – and then I felt if you were going to have to defend me you could do a better job if you . . . well, I thought it would perhaps rob you of some of your assurance if . . .'

Mason interrupted. 'I asked you repeatedly if you had left your apartment and every time you assured me that . . .'

'I know. Honestly, Mr Mason, if I had had any idea I dropped that purse where it could have been found . . . I'm sorry.'

'*You're* sorry,' Mason said indignantly. 'Why, you little . . .'

The lawyer took a deep breath, said more calmly. 'People are watching us. Nod your head as though the contents of that letter were just what you expected.'

She nodded her head.

Mason smilingly returned the letter to his briefcase, patted her encouragingly on the back, said under his breath, 'Well, you're in it now, and you've got me in it too.'

'I tell you he was dead when I got there.' she said. 'I . . .'

'You've already told enough lies,' Mason observed smilingly. 'Go back to your cell and keep your mouth shut. I'll try and salvage something from the wreckage, because I'm in a spot where I have to. You have me in this right along with you. No wonder Claud Gloster has been triumphant! I suppose he's even got a witness who saw you on the bus going back to town.'

Mason stood up, smiling confidently, picked up his briefcase, motioned to Paul Drake and Della Street.

'Keep smiling,' he said, as he walked out of the courtroom.

Newspaper reporters pressed him for a statement. Here and there spectators pushed forward to ask questions. Mason smilingly brushed them all to one side.

In the privacy of his automobile Paul Drake said, 'Gosh, Perry, you sure got the sheriff mixed up on those signatures, but that purse business looks pretty bad. Do you suppose she actually did go down there and double-crossed you ?'

'She double-crossed everyone, including herself,' Mason said angrily. 'She went down there.'

'Good lord!' Della Street exclaimed.

'Now then,' Mason said, 'we have between now and ten o'clock tomorrow morning to try and get out of this.'

'What can you do ?' Paul Drake asked.

Mason said, 'I don't know. They've hit us two body blows. The one which indicates that Dorothy Fenner was down there on the day of the murder is bad enough, but the other one is a stem winder.'

'You mean that newspaper clipping ?'

'That newspaper clipping. That contains an account of Alder having filed a complaint alleging that Dorothy Fenner broke into his place, stole fifty thousand dollars' worth of jewels, that she jumped in the water when she was pursued by the dog, and that a male accomplice was waiting for her in a canoe.

'The jury will, of course, be instructed to consider the newspaper clipping only for the purpose of showing the date at which the purse was dropped. But you know what a jury will do. They'll eat that stuff up.'

'Well, can't you show that . . .'. .

'The hell of it is, I can't,' Mason said. 'My hands are tied. I had been thinking all along that Claud Gloster would introduce that letter contained in the bottle which the police must have found when they went through George Alder's effects. I thought that he'd try to introduce the evidence of the burglary, claim that it was all part of the *res gestae* and, as his motive, claim that Dorothy Fenner had gone back there to try and get that letter.

'I was then prepared to crucify him by showing that Dorothy Fenner didn't need to go back to get the letter because she'd already made a copy of it, and that Dorley Alder had seen a copy of the letter before the murder was committed. That would knock the props out of the prosecution's motivation. Then I intended to drag enough evidence in about the death of Minerva Danby to make it appear that Alder was a murderer and had got just what was coming to him, and kick the prosecution's case all over the court-room, and then out of the window.

'Now, then, you can see what's happened. They're not going to bring that letter in. They'll even try and keep it out. It's up to me to try and bring it in, and they're going to claim that in place of being part of the *res gestae*, the letter is hearsay, incompetent, irrelevant, and immaterial.'

'Well, isn't it ?' Drake asked.

'In all probability it is,' Mason said, 'but I've got to dig up some theory by which I can at least *try* to get the thing before the court. And we don't know where the original letter is.'

'You have a copy,' Della Street said.

'I have a copy,' Mason told her, 'but we're going to have to get it authenticated. The only way to do that is to go down and see this man who found it, Pete Cadiz.'

'I know where we can locate him,' Drake said.

'I've been afraid to go near him before,' Mason said, 'because I didn't dare to let on to the prosecution that I knew about this letter. I wanted to let them think I was going to try to keep that letter out and . . . Gosh, what a mess!'

'Well,' Drake said, 'you can't be blamed for it, Perry.'

Mason said fervently, 'If that little devil could get on the witness-stand and lie one half as convincingly to the jury as she lied to me – but she won't and she can't. She'll go all to pieces and start bawling and having hysterics. I know the type. When she thinks everything is coming her way she can be dead game, but the minute the going gets tough she starts crying and seeking sympathy.

'I should have known better, but the way she looked me right in the eyes and swore by all that was holy that she'd been in her apartment all the evening, the way she accounted for her time, and – and now to have the whole thing blow up in my face, right in the middle of a jury trial.'

'Do you suppose she is guilty ?' Della Street asked.

'I can't even answer that question until after the evidence is all in,' Mason said. 'I wouldn't trust her word now on anything, and the hell of it is that I'm stuck with defending her.'

'I don't see why you're stuck with her,' Della Street said. 'After all, you . . .'

'After all,' Mason interrupted, 'I was the sucker who picked her up in the canoe Saturday night right after her escapade, and I'm afraid that Claud Gloster not only suspects it, but *may* have some evidence. It's been rumoured around the court-house that he's been bragging about having all thirteen trumps. We'll go see what Pete Cadiz has to say.'

Drake said, 'She could be telling the truth, Perry. But if she isn't, *I* think she could make out some sort of a case for self-defence.'

'There must have been one hell of a fight before Alder was bumped off. It wasn't simply a matter of somebody grabbing the gun from his desk and shooting him.

'One of my men got there and saw the scratches on the inside of that panelled closet door. He said you could see where the dog had been in a perfect frenzy, trying to get out. The scratches were all so fresh that there were still little splinters hanging to the places where the claw marks cut across the panels.'

Mason said thoughtfully, 'I've tried to figure out what happened, Paul. A man must have done the job, or else some woman who was struggling. There must have been a real knock-down, drag-out fight and then while they were struggling, this person grabbed the revolver. Of course, Dorothy Fenner *could* be telling the truth now, but after my experience with her, I'm afraid to trust her.'

'Well, whatever happened,' Drake said positively, 'I'm betting there was a long-drawn-out struggle. The dog had that door scratched to pieces.'

Mason said, 'We'll file that fact away for future reference. The way things are now I don't dare to plan a defence until I see what further surprises the prosecution may have for us. From now on I'll listen to the evidence as it comes in. Then I'll have to wind up knowing *just* how that crime was committed – and make everyone think I knew it before I consented to take Dorothy Fenner's case.'

CHAPTER SIXTEEN

The sunset hush had settled like a mantle over the still water as Mason, Della Street, and Paul Drake walked out over the echoing planks, studying the forest of stubby masts which from time to time swayed gently in the little swells made by the passing of an occasional speedboat.

From somewhere in the distance came the sound of an accordion, and a cracked baritone voice singing a sentimental ballad of a bygone era. Then the singing ceased, but the accordion played on.

'I think,' Drake said, 'that's our man. He's supposed to spend an hour or so every night playing over some of the old tunes. The story goes that he was very much in love with a girl who died, and now he lives alone, true to her memory and playing the songs he sang while he was courting her. If you serve that subpoena on him, Perry, think of what a sob sister could do with the story. That's your angle for getting the stuff about the bottle letter into the Press.'

'I don't want it in the Press,' Mason said, 'I want it in evidence – and the way I feel about my client right now I wouldn't doubt but what she did grab some jewellery on that Saturday night. . . . Well' we'll have to wait and see what other unpleasant surprises Claud Gloster has in store for us.'

They walked along the long pier until finally they made out the form of a grizzled seaman, sitting in the bow of a trim fishing boat, playing the accordion, his face, granite hard from wind and salt spray, etched with deep lines.

Della Street put a restraining hand on Mason's arm, whispered, 'Wait until he finishes.'

Drake turned, caught her eye, and she gently shook her head.

The three of them stood in the lee of a weather-beaten shed all but invisible in the shadows, watching the dim figure of the man in the boat below, listening to old tunes which had been popular forty years ago.

At length the number was finished. The man eased his accordion to his lap, raised his head, and looked out towards the west where the last tint of colour was fading, leaving an evening star in sole possession of the sky; an evening star so bright that the reflection of it made a shimmering thread of gold in the water.

The man heard their steps as they moved forward, looked up and watched them curiously.

Mason, in the lead, introduced himself and his companions. Cadiz studied them, nodded, and turned back towards the western sky for a moment.

Della Street said sympathetically, 'It's romantic, isn't it, out here on the water in the twilight?'

Cadiz nodded.

'We wanted to ask you some questions about that bottle.' Mason said. 'The one you found with the letter in it.'

Cadiz looked at him and said nothing.

Della Street said impulsively, 'I presume you don't feel much like talking after living with those old memories, and . . .'

Suddenly Cadiz stepped to the rail and shot a stream of tobacco juice down into the water, then he turned back to them and said, 'It ain't that, ma'am, it's that damned tobacco juice. What about the bottle?'

Paul Drake caught Mason's eye. Della Street, intercepting the glance, smiled, and Mason said, 'I want to know just exactly what happened. I want to know all about how you happened to find that bottle, where it was, and what you did with it.

Pete Cadiz thought for a moment, then spat the quid of tobacco over the side, ran his tongue around his teeth to clear his mouth, spat once more, turned and faced his visitors.

'I'm independent. I don't like civilisation.'

'Who does?' Mason asked, grinning.

'Well,' Cadiz said, 'the way I figure things out, a man gets to playing around too much with civilisation and he gets taxed one way and another so much he has to keep working harder to make more money to get taxed more.'

'Income tax bothering you?' Mason asked.

'Not the income tax, just the tax that civilisation puts on a person. You have a poor job, you make a little money. You get a better job and you have to start wearing good clothes. Then you have cleaning bills and laundry bills. Then you have to work harder in order to get a better job to pay for that, and by the time you've done that you have to start entertaining, and that means you need a house and have to have a car. Then you work harder and you get a better job . . .'

'Don't,' Paul Drake grinned. 'You're killing me.'

Pete Cadiz ran an eye up and down Paul Drake's well-dressed figure and said, 'The hell I am. You're killing yourself.'

'Go on,' Mason said, his voice showing his interest. 'What do *you* do, Pete?'

Cadiz said, '*I* do as I damn please.'

'You might give us the formula,' Drake said.

'I'm telling you,' Cadiz said, 'I've been through the mill. I started out in the packing department of a big plant, moving boxes around. Then I studied salesmanship in my spare time and got to be a salesman. Then I got to be assistant sales manager. Then I got to be sales manager. Then I had ulcers and then I fell in love and . . . oh, hell, what's the use.'

He turned back towards the ocean, stood at the rail looking down into the dark, swirling waters. Then he swung back once more to face his visitors. 'Okay, I said to hell with the whole business. I didn't have anything left by the time I got my debts paid except a few five-dollar ties, some silk shirts, a collection of pyjamas, five tailor-made suits and . . . well, you can draw the picture yourself.'

'Well, now the letter,' Drake said, 'was . . .'

Mason nudged him with his elbow and Drake became abruptly quiet.

'Well,' Cadiz said, 'I found a boat that was for sale. I had a few commissions coming to me and I managed to finance the boat out of the commissions. I didn't have much left to live on. People talked to me about going into the commercial fishing business. Then I needed a crew, I needed gasoline, I needed ice – and I asked them what I did with the fish after I caught them, and they told me I sold them, of course; so then I asked them what I did with the money, and they explained to me that I used the money to buy food, get more gasoline, pay off the crew and catch more fish.'

'So what did you do?' Mason asked.

'So I just started out by myself, and because I was my own crew I didn't have to pay me. Then when I caught fish, instead of selling them to the public to eat and taking the money for the fish to buy food, I bought the fish from myself, but since I owed the money to me I didn't have to pay anything. And then I ate the fish.'

'Sounds simple,' Mason said.

'The hell of it is,' Cadiz observed, 'it *is* simple.'

'How long have you been doing this?' Mason asked.

'Long enough to get rid of the ulcers and get happy and healthy. Now the point that I'm getting at is that since I have what you might call a close-coupled economy with myself, working for myself, employing myself, getting wages from myself, selling fish to myself, and . . .'

'Don't you need *any* money?' Paul Drake asked.

'Well,' Pete Cadiz pointed out, 'there isn't a great deal of outside money comes in, so I aim to be pretty self-sufficient. I make a few lobster traps and when I get ready to make them I don't have money to go buy lumber. I find my lumber in the form of driftwood. I get around and catch abalones, sell some abalone-shell ornaments, I pick up odd bits of driftwood, sell a few knick-knacks here and there to yachtsmen. I drift around wherever I happen to want to be. Sometimes I have to pour some gasoline into the engine, but for the most part I use the wind. The wind is free and it'll get you there. Not always on schedule, but what the hell is a schedule? Living the sort of life I live you don't have to worry about clocks and calendars.'

Mason nodded.

'Well,' Cadiz went on, 'there's a little half-moon bay below here that's sandy and shaped just right to catch a lot of drift. I don't know exactly why it is, except that the currents, the wind, and the way the tide sets keep that little cove piled full of drift stuff. If there's anything drifting around it'll come into this cove.

'There'll be a hell of a surf running in there and quite a tide when there's a storm out at sea, but when it's quiet you can slide in there in a skiff, if you know how to handle a skiff. You'll always find stuff in there that you can use in making lobster traps. You'll get driftage, salvage, firewood, and all that stuff.

'Well I was making some lobster traps and I had a spell of calm weather for about a week. I anchored my boat offshore and I'd row in and out with my skiff, just combing the beach, picking up stuff and ferrying it out to my boat.'

'How big a cove?' Mason asked.

'Just a tiny little place nestled down in some hills. Not many people know about it. Well, I was prowling along the edge of the tide line, looking pretty sharp because I'd just about combed the place clean, and then I happened to see this bottle. I took a look at it and saw it had been corked up and turned adrift, and there was a letter of some sort in it and I could look through the glass and see that it was on the stationery of the *Thayerbelle*.

'Well, I get around where the yachtsmen are quite a bit. They get a kick out of me. Some of them feel sorry for me. Poor devils, if they knew how sorry I felt for them, holding their noses on the grindstone and running like hell in the economic treadmill to keep the grindstone turning faster and faster.

'Well, anyway, I know most of the yachtsmen. I sell them stuff: bait, and lobsters, and sometimes an interesting bit of driftage, and abalone-shell soap-dishes, and things of that sort. I guess I know as many yachtsmen as anyone on the coast, and they know me and like me.

'Well, I had about combed this little beach out, so I got in my yacht and sailed up to San Diego and went to a telephone and put through a call collect to George Alder. I told him I had a bottle with some sort of a letter in it that evidently had been kicked overboard from his yacht. He didn't seem much interested at first and then he began to get curious and he suggested that I bring the bottle in to him and he'd pay me for my time and trouble.

'Well . . . well, I did it.'

'And what happened?' Mason asked.

'Well, he took the letter out of the bottle and read it, and then he gave me fifty bucks. Then he asked me if I'd read the letter and I told him it wasn't my business to read letters but only to pick up bottles, and then he gave me a hundred bucks.'

Cadiz turned away, and once more looked down at the ocean.

Mason waited for several seconds, but the man didn't turn back to face him. The silence became embarrassing.

'How was that bottle buried?' Mason asked.

'Sort of on a slant, half in the sand and half out, and the part that was out had all roughened up from sand blowing on the wind – you know, the way glass will when it's exposed to sand blown by wind, sort of a ground-glass effect.'

'So Alder gave you fifty dollars?'

'That's right.'

'And then after a while made it a hundred?'

'Uh-huh . . . a hundred more.'

Mason said, 'Alder's dead now. You *could* be released of your obligations to him, Pete.'

'What do you mean?'

Mason said, 'I mean this, Pete, that if you had just picked up the bottle the way you said, you'd have put it in your boat some place and the next time you happened to be over around the yachts and saw the *Thayerbelle* anchored there you'd have got in your skiff, rowed over to pass the time of day with Alder, and casually mentioned this bottle you'd found. A man who has shaken the shackles of civilisation the way you have doesn't go around telephoning collect because he finds a bottle and . . .'

Cadiz whirled around to face him. 'You mean I'm lying?' he demanded belligerently.

Mason measured the man with his eyes, brushed the belligerency aside with a disarming smile and said good-naturedly, 'Pete, you're not only lying but you're making an awful job of it. Is doesn't come natural to you.'

Cadiz took a swift step towards the lawyer, then suddenly the anger left him and his pugnaciousness evaporated, a slow grin twisted his face. 'Okay,' he said, 'you're doing the talking.'

Mason said. 'My best guess is, Pete, that you read that letter in order to see what it was, and *after* you'd read it you knew that Alder would be interested in it so you took it in to him and it was after Alder found out that you had read the letter that he gave you the extra hundred dollars and made you promise that you'd forget all about it.'

'You're doing the talking,' Cadiz said.

'What would you do if you got on the witness-stand?' Mason asked.

Cadiz thought that over for a while, then said, 'Well, you're a pretty smart lawyer. I ain't saying anything right now. *If* I'd made any sort of a deal with George Alder, I'd try to live up to it, but nothing was said about getting on the witness-stand. If I got on the witness-stand and . . . Hell, I'd tell the truth.'

Mason pulled a folded paper from his pocket. 'Cadiz,' he said, 'this is a subpoena which I am serving on you, a subpoena ordering you to appear in court tomorrow morning at ten o'clock to testify on behalf of the defendent in the case of The People of the State of California versus Dorothy Fenner. Now, we won't be able to use you tomorrow morning, but you'll have to be in court in accordance with the terms of this subpoena. You're a witness

131

for the defence, and there isn't any reason for you to tell anyone about this talk or what you're supposed to testify to. Now, while I can't give you any more money than is allowed by law without it appearing that I'm trying to influence you, I can give you mileage which will bring you to court and you'll be paid an amount which will compensate you for your loss of time.'

Cadiz took the subpoena, folded it, pushed it down into his trousers pocket and said, 'That's the hell of getting mixed up with civilisation. I thought that hundred and fifty dollars was a little too easy.'

'You'll be there ?' Mason asked.

'I'll be there,' Cadiz said. 'I'm going to hate the thing all to hell, but I'll be there.'

CHAPTER SEVENTEEN

The crowded court-room was charged with an atmosphere of excitement.

Claud Gloster, appreciating to the full the dramatic possibilities of the moment, arose as soon as court had convened and said, 'Your Honour, we have a witness under subpoena, a Ronald Dixon, whose duties are such that it becomes necessary for him to be excused at as early an hour as possible. I would, therefore, ask permission of Court and Counsel to temporarily withdraw the sheriff from the stand and put on Mr Ronald Dixon out of order.'

'Any objection ?' Judge Garey asked Mason.

Mason was smiling, confident, as one who is magnanimous in victory.

'No objection whatever, Your Honour.'

'Very well, on the strength of the district attorney's statement that it is necessary for this witness to be called out of order, and since no objection is made by the defence, it will be so ordered.'

Ronald Dixon, tall, studious, slightly stooped, came towards the witness-stand and Mason, catching a quick glimpse of the man's profile as he walked by, whispered to Della Street, 'I've seen that man before.'

He turned to his left and said to Dorothy Fenner, 'Do you know this man ?'

'Night clerk at the apartment,' she said.

Mason grinned. 'Here's where they prove Alder's visit.'

Ronald Dixon was sworn, gave his name, age, residence and occupation, settled himself in the witness-chair as though he expected to be there for a long time and was making himself as comfortable as possible.

'You're acquainted with the defendant, Dorothy Fenner?' Gloster asked.

'Yes, sir.'

'You have stated that you are one of the night clerks at the Monadnock Hotel Apartments?'

'Yes, sir.'

'What are your hours?'

'From four in the afternoon until twelve o'clock midnight.'

'On the third of August of this year were you so employed and working those hours?'

'Yes, sir.'

'And did at that time?'

'Yes, sir.'

'Now, Mr Dixon, directing your attention to the late afternoon of the third, will you tell us what happened of your own knowledge with reference to Miss Fenner's apartment?'

'Well, I had read in the paper that she'd been . . .'

'Never mind that, never mind that,' Gloster interrupted. 'Just what you know of your own knowledge.'

'Yes, sir. Well, she came in about five-thirty, I guess it was, about an hour or so after I'd come on and started work, and I congratulated her on . . .'

'You had a conversation?' Gloster interrupted quickly.

'That's right. I talked with her and she . . .'

'Then what happened?' Gloster interrupted again. 'What did she do?'

'She asked if there was any mail and I told her there had been about a million telephone calls and she took all the notes out of her key-box, and then went over to the elevator to go up to her apartment.'

'Then what?'

'Then about an hour later a gentleman came in and said he wanted to see her. He told me she was expecting him, so there was no need to announce him. Well, that's against the rules of the place, but he looked like the sort of man you could trust – reserved, a gentleman – not the sort that would be apt to make any racket, cause any trouble or report a man for violating a rule.'

'So what did you do ?' Gloster asked.

'Well, I sort of hesitated, and then he handed me a five-dollar note.'

'So then what did you do ?'

Dixon grinned and said, 'So I did nothing.'

'Meaning that you did not announce him ?'

'That's right. I let him go on up.'

'Now, did you get a good look at that man ?'

'I had a very good look at him.'

'Would you know him if you saw him again ?'

'Yes, sir.'

'*Did* you see him again ?'

'Yes, sir.'

'Where ?'

'Lying on a slab at the undertaker's.'

'In other words, this man was George S. Alder ?'

'I was informed that was his name.'

'I show you a photograph, Mr Dixon, and ask you if you recognise this photograph.'

'Yes, sir.'

'Who is it ?'

'That's a photograph of the man who came to see Dorothy Fenner that afternoon and gave me the five dollars.'

'And what time was this ?'

'Oh, I'd say it was about probably around six-thirty.'

'How long was this man up there, do you know ?'

Mason said, 'He doesn't know that the man ever went to the defendant's apartment. All he knows is that the man gave him five dollars and said that he wanted to see the defendant. That conversation isn't binding on the defendant. Unless you connect it up in some way. I'll move to strike it all out.'

'I'll connect it up,' Gloster said grimly.

'Very well, proceed,' Judge Garey said.

'Well,' Dixon observed, grinning slightly, 'if the man didn't go to see Dorothy Fenner, he wasted a five-dollar investment.'

The court-room broke into laughter.

Judge Garey, pounding with his gavel, said, 'That will do. The witness will not volunteer any comments.'

'Go ahead,' Gloster said, a wide smile on his face. 'Tell us exactly what the man did that you saw.'

'Well, he gave me five dollars. He went over to the elevator. He punched the button. He got in the elevator. He closed the doors and the elevator went up, and about forty minutes later the man came down and said, "Thank you" to me and walked out.'

Mason laced his fingers back of his head, tilted back in the swivel chair and smiled good-naturedly. Now that his case had collapsed in a mass of legal wreckage, he was like a fighter in a corner, trying to measure the strength of his antagonist, to find some way of escape. However, his manner was that of one who is completely certain of himself, confident of the outcome.

And the fact that Gloster had considered this witness important enough to be put on out of order, yet only to bring out a fact with which Mason was fully familiar, made the lawyer feel that perhaps the district attorney might not hold such high trumps after all.

Mason kept his expression of smiling confidence, but permitted himself a sigh of relief.

Then suddenly his stomach tightened as he heard Gloster shoot in the next question.

'Now then, did you see the defendant leaving the apartment house later on during the evening?'

'Yes, sir.'

'Under what circumstances, please?'

'Well, I'd left the desk temporarily, just stepped out of the little office there for a moment, and as I returned I saw the figure of a woman walking rather quickly across the lobby and towards the street door. That woman was Dorothy Fenner.'

'And what time was this?'

'About seven-thirty in the evening.'

'That was the evening of the third?'

'Yes, sir.'

'Now, did you have occasion to see the defendant again on that evening?'

'Yes, sir.'

'When?'

'When she came back.'

'What do you mean by that?'

'Well, there are some doors we keep locked. We lock the outside door to the lobby at night, but any of the tenants can open that door. The key to any of the apartments opens it. The baggage room is the same way. It opens on the alley. It's kept locked, but any tenant can use his key to get in. But when that door gets opened an electric signal tells us at the desk. A buzzer and a little red flashlight come on at intervals. In that way we know when anyone's come in from the outside through the trunk-room.'

135

'Very well, what happened?'

'Well, this buzzer and the light I'm telling you about came on about eleven-thirty. I thought I'd better investigate. I left the desk and started towards the stairs to the trunk-room. While I was doing that, I heard the elevator coming down the shaft. Someone had signalled for it. I ran down the stairs, opened the door a crack, and saw the defendant standing there waiting for the elevator.'

'How close were you to the defendant?'

'Not over ten feet.'

'You recognised her?'

'Definitely.'

'Any chance you were mistaken?'

'No, sir.'

'How was she dressed?'

'She had on a white sweater, some sort of blue dungarees that she usually wears for yachting, and a pair of tennis shoes.'

'And what happened?'

'The elevator came to a stop, the defendant got in and closed the door. I ran back upstairs to the lobby and noticed the indicator hand on the elevator. It went to the fourth floor and stopped.'

'And the defendant's apartment is on the fourth floor?'

'Yes, sir.'

'Now, had you any means of knowing whether or not the defendant was in her apartment between the hours of seven o'clock in the evening and ten o'clock in the evening of that day?'

'Yes, sir.'

'Explain, please.'

'Well, I have to make an inventory every three months of things in the apartments the tenants had to sign for. I'd been wanting to get up to the defendant's apartment, so when I saw her go out I rang the night housekeeper and said now was the time to check on the apartment. I told her Miss Fenner was out. I'd already told Miss Fenner we'd check her apartment, some time when she wasn't there so it wouldn't disturb her. She said that was okay, to go ahead.'

'So what happened?'

'So I told the housekeeper to go on up like I just told you. I said Miss Fenner was out.'

'Do you know whether the housekeeper did or not?'

'Sure, She told me . . .'

'Well, never mind. We'll prove that by the housekeeper,'

Gloster said. 'Now, there is one more question. How was the defendant dressed when she went out?'

'She wore a light plaid skirt with jacket to match. I noticed that much about the way she was dressed when she went out, but I didn't see her until after she'd left the elevator and was walking towards the door, so I was looking at her back. I don't know what colour blouse she had on. But I do know she'd changed her clothes while she was out. She went out wearing a skirt and returned in a sweater and dungarees.'

'Would you recognise the skirt she was wearing if you saw it again?'

'I would, yes, sir.'

'Now, then,' Gloster said triumphantly, 'I refer you to the People's Exhibit D, the skirt and jacket which the sheriff has testified were found on board the yacht owned by the defendant, the *Kathy-Kay*, and ask you if you have ever seen these garments before.'

'Yes, sir, those are the things that Dorothy Fenner, the defendant, wore when she left the apartment.'

'And when she came back she wasn't wearing those things?'

'No, sir, she was wearing her yachting clothes, a white turtle-necked knit sweater and yachting slacks and tennis shoes.'

'Now, did you notice anything about whether she was carrying a purse when she left the apartment?'

'Yes, sir, she was carrying her purse with her when she left the apartment house that night. I distinctly remember seeing the purse in her right hand.'

'And did she carry a purse when she returned and had the elevator brought down to the trunk-room?'

'No, sir, she did not.'

Gloster turned to Perry Mason with something of a smirk. 'Now, then, Mr Mason, go ahead and cross-examine.'

Mason said casually, as though the testimony of the witness had not surprised him with a series of body blows, 'Oh, I have just a few questions. Just a moment, please.'

Mason, smiling affably, arose from his chair. His eyes were amused and tolerant, as he said, 'As I understand it from your testimony, it was against the rules to permit Mr Alder to go up to the apartment unannounced?'

'Yes, sir.'

'But you did it?'

'Yes, sir.'

137

'For five dollars ?'

'Well, if you want to put it that way, yes.'

'A violation of the rules for five dollars,' Mason said, smiling.

The witness said defiantly, 'All right.'

'Would you,' Mason asked. 'have done it for four ?'

There was a ripple of laughter in the court-room.

The witness was stubbornly silent.

'Would you ?' Mason asked.

'Oh, Your Honour,' Gloster said, 'I object to that. The question is argumentative and it's not proper cross-examination.'

'Well, I suppose it is argumentative,' Judge Garey ruled, 'but I think it's within the scope of proper cross-examination.'

'Would you have done it for four ?' Mason asked.

'I suppose so,' the witness said sullenly.

'For three ?'

'Yes!' he shouted angrily.

'For two ?'

'I don't know.' The witness was sullen again.

'For one ?'

'*No !*'

Mason said, 'Thank you, Mr Dixon, I was just getting the value which you place on your honour.'

Mason held the witness with his eyes, but the margin of his consciousness told him what was going on, the amusement of the spectators in the court-room, the anger of the district attorney.

'Now, then,' Mason said, 'when the defendant came in on the afternoon of the third, you had some conversation with her ?'

'Yes, sir.'

'You told her there were about a million telephone calls ?'

'Yes. Of course that was a figure of speech.'

'Exactly,' Mason said. 'A witness who is as scrupulously careful of the truth as you are wouldn't want the jury to believe that you had actually packed a million telephone slips into an ordinary key-box.'

Mason's smile was affable.

The witness squirmed.

'Now, then,' Mason said, 'you had some little talk with the defendant at that time ?'

'Oh . . . yes, I guess we did.'

'About how long did that conversation take ?' Mason asked. 'How long was she standing there chatting with you ?'

'About five minutes, I would judge.'

'And then she took the elevator and went up in the elevator ?'

'That's right.'

'That was an automatic-elevator ?'

'Yes, sir.'

'And how long was this before this gentleman came in – the gentleman who gave you the five dollars for violating the rules ?'

Dixon flushed.

'How long was it ?'

'Oh, I would say it was about an hour or an hour and a half, something like that.'

'And how long before you saw the defendant going out ?'

'Well, she went out about forty minutes after the man who had been to see her left – I guess . . . well, you can figure it out.'

'Now, then,' Mason said, 'just tell the jury exactly what you and the defendant talked about during this five-minute conversation, exactly what you said to her.'

'Your Honour,' Gloster shouted, jumping to his feet, 'that is incompetent, irrelevant, and immaterial; it's not part of the *res gestae*; it's not proper cross-examination; it calls for a self-serving declaration, and it's utterly outside of the issues in this case.'

'Unless counsel can show that it has some specific bearing on the case,' Judge Garey said.

Mason smiled and said, 'I believe, Your Honour, it is a rule of law that, when a witness on direct examination is asked as to a part of a conversation, the cross-examiner has the right to bring out the entire conversation.'

'That's right,' Judge Garey said. 'That is the general rule.'

'And I have no fault to find with it,' Gloster said, 'which is the reason I was so careful to interrupt the witness every time he started to talk about that conversation. I didn't want him to testify to it because I think it has no bearing on the case.'

'But,' Mason said, 'you *did* ask him about the conversation, and he answered the question.'

'That is not true!' Gloster shouted. 'I was particularly care-ful . . .'

'You asked the witness about what happened, and he told you that he told the defendant there were about a million telephone calls in her box – and I just asked the witness that question all over again to make sure there was no misunderstanding.'

Gloster, suddenly embarrassed, said lamely, 'That's not a conversation.'

'Well, it's not a correspondence, it's not clairvoyance, and it's not telepathy. I don't know what it is, if it isn't a conversation,' Mason retorted.

Judge Garey frowned, then slowly nodded. 'I guess,' he said, 'that opens the door, if counsel for the defence wants to go into it.'

'Your Honour,' Gloster said, 'I happen to know what is back of all this. If we open this door, we will drag in innumerable and interminable side issues.'

'You should have thought of it before you opened the door then,' Judge Garey said. 'Go ahead and answer the question.'

'Give all the conversation as nearly as you can,' Mason said to the witness, 'what you said to her, and what she said to you.'

'Oh, Your Honour,' Gloster said, 'this is . . .'

'The objection has been made, and a ruling has also been made,' Judge Garey pointed out, tartly.

'Your Honour, might I ask for a recess at this time? I think that . . . I would like to argue the matter with the Court outside of the hearing of the jury.'

'*We* have nothing to conceal,' Mason said. 'If there was a conversation, we want it.'

'All right,' Gloster said angrily. 'I warn you that you may be able to get the conversation in, but that isn't going to open the door so that you can prove any of the things that were mentioned in the conversation. We're going to object to anything coming into this case except the question of the murder of George S. Alder.'

'Why, certainly,' Mason said.

'Go ahead,' Judge Garey said to the witness, 'answer the question. What was said?'

'Well,' Dixon said, 'I congratulated her on having been released, and she told me that Mr Alder had gone all to pieces under Mr Mason's cross-examination, and that the charge he had made that she had stolen some jewellery from him couldn't be substantiated, and that he couldn't even describe what the jewellery was; that it was quite a triumph for her, and that she had an idea Mr Alder would be trying to squirm out of a very embarrassing situation.'

Gloster, thoroughly angry, said, 'Your Honour, I want an instruction to the jury that this testimony is merely as to a conversation between the defendant and this witness, that the fact the defendant may have *made* a certain self-serving declaration is no proof of the truth of the facts therein mentioned.'

Mason said quite affably, as befits a victorious antagonist, 'I

140

take it that the district attorney is merely stating his contentions ?'

'I'm pointing out what the law is,' Gloster shouted.

'Well, you don't need to educate *me* on the law,' Mason said, smiling. 'So far, the shoe has been on the other foot, and I'm quite certain that the Court knows more law than you do.'

A gale of laughter swept the court-room. Judge Garey smiled, but perfunctorily rapped the gavel. 'Come, come, gentlemen, let's have some semblance of order here, and we'll try to refrain from personalities.'

'I want the jury instructed, however, that this conversation is only a conversation,' Gloster said.

'A moment ago the district attorney was contending that it was *not* a conversation,' Mason said.

Before the confused district attorney could get his mental feet under him, Mason went on, 'Furthermore, Your Honour, on behalf of the defence I want certain bits of evidence produced for our inspection. If the prosecution is holding any papers that were taken from the desk of the decedent, we want an opportunity to inspect those papers.'

Judge Garey raised his eyebrows. 'Do you mean by that to ask for an inspection of the prosecution's evidence in advance ?'

'Not of the prosecution's *evidence*,' Mason said, 'but there are certain things, certain papers which I believe would be evidence for the defence, and which I have reason to believe the prosecution has taken from the desk of the decedent and is holding, merely for the purpose of keeping the defendant from having access to them.'

Judge Garey looked questioningly at Gloster.

'I do not know what counsel is referring to,' Gloster said, 'and I'm going to state here and now that we are only holding matters which we intend to introduce in evidence, and we are certainly under no obligation to show such evidence to the defence.'

'Provided it *is* evidence, and provided you introduce it,' Mason said.

'Well, we're holding evidence, and the things we're holding are held for evidence.'

'But suppose you should change your mind and decide not to introduce them.'

'That's our privilege.'

'Then we want the privilege of inspecting them,' Mason said.

Gloster, starting to present his position at length, was interrupted by Mason saying suavely to the Court, 'And, of course,

Your Honour, the Court itself will notice the tactics of the prosecution in trying to suppress evidence.'

'What do you mean by making charges like that!' Gloster stormed. 'That's professional misconduct. We haven't suppressed anything. We . . .'

'Tut, tut,' Mason interrupted chidingly, 'you remember that the Court instructed you to tell us where the dog was, and you haven't done so.'

Gloster yelled, 'I told you I didn't know. I told you that the sheriff . . .'

'Just a moment,' Judge Garey interrupted. 'Counsel for the defence is quite correct on that. The order of the Court was that you were to communicate to the defence where the dog was being held.'

'I didn't so understand it,' Gloster said, suddenly embarrassed. 'I made the statement that *I* didn't know where the dog was being kept, but that the sheriff did, and when the sheriff was on the stand, counsel for the defence had every opportunity to ask him, and failed to do so.'

Mason said, 'The Court's order was that you were to tell us where the dog was kept.'

'That was the intent of the Court's order,' Judge Garey said.

'Well, I didn't so understand it.'

'Well, where *is* the dog?' Mason asked.

'I . . . well, I can't tell you where he is now. I can tell you where he was.'

'Why can't you tell me where he is now?' Mason asked.

'Because,' Gloster said, angrily, 'I'm not going to hand our entire case to you on a silver platter so that you can start picking it to pieces. The dog was taken to the Acme Boarding Kennels, but one of our witnesses wanted to take the dog and did so. And the dog is staying with her. I can't give you the address of the dog without giving the address of the witness, and I don't care to have you tampering with our witnesses.'

'What are you afraid of?' Mason asked. 'Do you think I'd get her to tell a lie? Would she perjure herself at my request?'

'Of course not.'

'Then,' Mason said, smiling at the jury, 'you must be afraid that I'd get her to tell the *truth*.'

'Your Honour,' Gloster protested, 'this is all getting far afield. We're getting this case in a mess because we're trying to pursue a lot of collateral matters.'

'I merely wanted to know where the dog was,' Mason asked cheerfully, 'and the Court told you to tell me. Now you're trying to squirm out from under the order of the Court.'

'I'm not trying to do any such thing.' You . . .'

Judge Garey pounded with his gavel, and said, 'Gentlemen, let's cease having these interchanges between counsel. Let's refrain from all personalities, and from now on counsel can each address the Court and not address opposing counsel.'

'Very well,' Mason said quickly, before Gloster could interpose any comment. 'One other thing that the defence wants is an order permitting the defence and the defence experts to inspect the scene of the crime. If the Court please, we have been barred from these premises and have been refused permission even to inspect them in order to prepare our defence.'

Judge Garey frowned. 'The defence certainly are entitled to inspect the premises.'

'The defendant had an opportunity to inspect them while she was murdering George Alder,' Gloster said.

'And I'll assign that remark as prejudicial misconduct on the part of the district attorney,' Mason said, 'and ask the Court to admonish the jury to disregard such remark and . . .'

'I'll withdraw the remark,' Gloster said contritely. 'I was angry. The remark was made in the heat of the discussion.'

'Well,' Judge Garey said, 'the Court will make an order that you and your experts may have a right to inspect the premises, Mr Mason. What time would be convenient ?'

'This afternoon ?' Mason asked.

'Oh, if the Court please,' Gloster protested, 'we've just started in with this case. If counsel is permitted to go out and inspect the premises this afternoon, we won't be able to resume testimony in the case until Monday.'

As the Court hesitated, Mason said, 'I have repeatedly requested the sheriff to permit experts for the defence to see these premises.'

'Permission which should have been granted,' the Court remarked. 'The Court will adjourn at twelve o'clock noon until Monday morning at ten o'clock. During the afternoon, and during tomorrow, which is Saturday, the Court will make an order that the defence may be admitted to the premises at all reasonable times, subject, of course, to the right of the prosecution to have officers there to maintain supervision. Now, then, gentlemen, are you finished with this witness, and, if so, are there any other witnesses ?'

Mason smiled at the discomfited man on the stand, and said, 'Oh, I guess as far as I'm concerned I have no further cross-examination. I think the jury understands the situation.'

'No questions,' Gloster said angrily, 'but since counsel is having so much fun I'll call a witness that will . . .'

'That will do,' Judge Garey interrupted. 'I have repeatedly admonished counsel to refrain from these comments. A continued and persistent refusal to follow the instructions of the Court will result in drastic action. Now, gentlemen, let's proceed with the trial of this case in an orderly manner. Mr District Attorney, call your next witness.'

CHAPTER EIGHTEEN

Gloster, on his feet, jaw thrust forward, said belligerently, 'My next witness is Oscar Linden. Oscar Linden, take the stand.'

Linden, a tall, loose-limbed, middle-aged man with a tattooed star plainly visible on the back of his left hand, took the witness-stand and after the usual preliminaries, Gloster started a barrage of quick, pounding questions.

'What's your occupation, Mr Linden?'

'I operate the boathouse at the Yacht Club.'

'And were you doing that on the first of August of this year? That was a Saturday, you'll remember.'

'Yes, sir.'

'Did you have occasion on that date, or very shortly afterwards, to look over the canoes you had rented during the evening?'

'Yes, sir.'

'How many canoes had you rented that night?'

'Twelve.'

'How many of them were back at the hour of ten o'clock?'

'Eight.'

'That left four out at that time?'

'Yes, sir.'

'Now, of those canoes – those four canoes, was there anything distinctive about any one of them?'

'Yes, sir.'

'What?'

'As a special de luxe service I have carpets which I put on the bottom of the canoes.'

'Did you notice anything peculiar about any of these canoes when it was returned?'

'Yes, sir.'

'What?'

'There was considerable water on the top of the carpet and in the bottom of one of the canoes. It was one numbered 0961. The number was painted on it in green paint.'

'What did you do with reference to that?'

'Nothing at the time, but shortly after Alder's murder I was in touch with the authorities. They wanted to go over my stock of canoes.'

'Now then, within the next two or three days did you make any further investigation?'

'Yes, sir.'

'What?'

'I turned this canoe over to a fingerprint expert at the request of the sheriff.'

'And do you keep a name list of the people who rent the canoes?'

'No, sir, I do not. There are numbers on the canoes and I keep a record of the numbers on those canoes. We charge either by the hour, by the evening, or by the half day.'

'How was this particular canoe in question rented?'

'By the evening. The person who rented it was entitled to stay out until one-thirty in the morning.'

'After you rented that canoe when did you next see it?'

'When I found it tied up to my dock next morning.'

'Up to the time that you turned that canoe over to the fingerprint expert and after it had been rented that evening, had anyone else been in the canoe?'

'Not to my knowledge.'

'Had it been rented?'

'No.'

'Now then, would you know the person who rented that canoe from you again, if you saw him?'

'Yes, sir.'

'Do you see that person?'

The boatman promptly pointed his finger at Perry Mason, and said, 'Mr Mason, the attorney there.'

'Cross-examine,' Gloster said.

'No questions,' Mason said, smiling affably, to the puzzlement of the jury and spectators. 'There can be no question but what I rented *a* canoe from this gentleman.'

Gloster said, 'Call Sam Durham to the stand.'

Sam Durham took the stand and qualified himself as an expert on fingerprints.

'Now then,' Gloster said, 'did you have occasion some time after the third of August to examine a canoe marked with the numerals 0961 in green paint on the bow and stern in a search for fingerprints?'

'I did, yes, sir.'

'What did you find?'

'I found numerous latent fingerprints which I photographed.'

'Subsequently did you identify any of those fingerprints?'

'I did, yes, sir.'

'What ones did you identify?'

'I identified certain latents which I have here in photographs numbered one, four, six and eight.'

'Whose fingerprints were they?'

'The fingerprints of the defendant.'

'Did you subsequently identify any of the other fingerprints?'

'At the time I was unable to do so, but later I identified fingerprints two, three, five and seven as shown in these photographs.'

'And when did you make that identification?'

'Last night.'

'And whose fingerprints are they?'

There was a dramatic silence in the court-room as the witness turned to face Perry Mason. 'Those are the fingerprints of Perry Mason, the attorney for the defendant.'

Judge Garey pounded with his gavel, trying in vain to subdue the clamour in the court-room. Finally he declared a fifteen-minute recess as newspaper reporters, disregarding the admonition of the Court, streaked through the crowd and out of the doors searching for telephones from which they could rush the news to their papers.

One of the newspaper reporters who had hurriedly left the court-room for a telephone, came pushing his way back, bringing a photographer with him.

'How about a statement, Mr Mason?' he asked.

The photographer raised the camera and the glare of a flash-light etched the scene into momentary brilliance.

Mason's grin was completely carefree. 'What sort of a statement?' he asked.

'What's the effect of this evidence?'

'You mean the fingerprint evidence?'

'Of course.'

Mason grinned, and said, 'I rented a canoe. I left my fingerprints on that canoe. There's no question about that. I'd have stipulated it if the district attorney hadn't wanted to make such a grandstand.'

'But how about the fingerprints of the defendant?'

'Quite apparently,' Mason said, affably, 'the fingerprints of the defendant are on that canoe also.'

'Then do you admit that you picked up the defendant after she tried to steal . . .'

'Come, come,' Mason said 'let's be fair about the thing. In the first place there's no proof the defendant tried to steal anything, and in the second place, ask the district attorney how he intends to prove that the fingerprints *were made at the same time.*

'You might stick around for the next fifteen minutes,' Mason said, grinning broadly, 'and learn something about fingerprint testimony.'

'Don't think I won't,' the reporter said. 'Is that all the statement you have to make?'

'That's it,' Mason said. 'What more do you want?'

The reporter thought over Mason's statement. 'But the witness said the canoe hadn't been rented since you took it out.'

'Exactly,' Mason smiled, as though enjoying some joke which would soon be apparent to the reporter.

CHAPTER NINETEEN

The bailiff called in the jury.

Judge Garey returned from his chambers and settled himself on the bench.

Gloster said, 'I had finished my direct examination of the witness, Sam Durham.'

'Cross-examine,' Judge Garey said.

Mason said, with a quiet smile, 'You examined this canoe for fingerprints at what time, Mr Durham?'

'Well, it was the evening of the third. Very late in the evening.

Nearly midnight, and the examination continued over until the morning of the fourth.'

'Now the third was the night of the murder.'

'Yes, sir.'

'And you understand that the first was the night the canoe had been rented ?'

'Yes, sir.'

'Where did you find these fingerprints ?'

'In various places.'

'Now how long, in your opinion, would a fingerprint, that is a latent fingerprint, last on a surface of that nature ?'

'Well, it would depend somewhat on atmospheric conditions and various circumstances, but I would say that one could expect to find fingerprints over a four-day period.'

'You are prepared to state that those are my fingerprints ?' Mason asked.

'I have compared them with an inked card containing an authentic set of your fingerprints. There can be no question as to the points of identity. If you wish, I have prepared enlarged photographs, showing the . . .'

'No, thank you,' Mason said, smiling. 'I am not questioning the fingerprints. I am merely trying now to fix the time element.'

'Yes, sir.'

'So that some time within four days before the hour of midnight of the third of August you would say that I had handled that canoe.'

'Yes, sir.'

'It could have been any time up to four days before you examined the canoe for fingerprints ?'

'Yes sir.'

'It could have been before that ?'

'Conceivably it could have been, but I would say that around four days would be the extreme time that fingerprints would be preserved under those circumstances.'

'And some time within four days of the time you made the examination around midnight of the third, the defendant had also left her fingerprints on that canoe ?'

'Yes, sir.'

'Now my fingerprints could have been made at any time during that four-day period ?'

'Yes, sir.'

'As recently as ten minutes before you arrived to test the latents?'

'Well . . . I . . . I'm not prepared to say.'

'Why not?'

'Well I . . . I suppose that *could* have been the case.'

'And the fingerprints of the defendant could have been made at any time within the four-day period.'

'Yes, sir.'

'As much as four full days before you made your test?'

'Yes.'

'So,' Mason said, triumphantly, 'according to your own testimony the fingerprints of the defendant *could* have been made four days before you made your tests, and mine could have been made when I was looking the canoe over for evidence not more than ten minutes prior to the time you made your tests.'

'Your Honour, I object to that line of questioning. I object to that as assuming a fact not in evidence,' Gloster shouted. 'I object because there is no evidence and there can be no evidence indicating that Mr Perry Mason was looking that canoe over for evidence. Why, I can prove . . .'

Mason grinned broadly, and said, 'I was merely asking questions as to the time element.'

'I defy you to state in court and in front of this jury that you ever examined that canoe for evidence,' Gloster said. 'And if you did. I demand to know what caused you to . . .'

'Don't get excited,' Mason told him. 'My questions of this witness relate merely to the time element. I'm trying to find the margin of time. You would like to be very dramatic and make it appear that because my fingerprints and the fingerprints of the defendant are on the same object, they must have been made at the same time. All that I'm trying to show on cross-examination is that they could have been made at any time over a ninety-six-hour period and could have been made ninety-six hours apart. So if you want to put me in that canoe at the same time the defendant was in it, Mr District Attorney, you are going to have to do a lot more than that.'

Gloster's face showed that that phase of the case had dawned on him for the first time.

Mason turned back to the witness. 'Do you know, Mr Durham, that the authorities searched the apartment of this defendant for evidence?'

'Yes, sir. I was there.'

'And District Attorney Gloster was also there?'

'Yes, sir.'

'So that if you examined that apartment now, you could reasonably expect to find objects bearing the latent fingerprints of *both* the district attorney and of the defendant?'

'Why I . . . I guess so . . . yes . . . Only they would have been made at different times.'

'Exactly,' Mason said, smiling. 'And now, Your Honour, we're quite willing to adjourn until Monday morning.'

Judge Garey smiled. 'The Court will take a recess until Monday morning at ten o'clock.'

CHAPTER TWENTY

Sheriff Keddie, stiff with official anger, took the key from his pocket, unlocked the gate in the stone wall which enclosed the land side of the big house and said, 'Now, I'm a busy man. I haven't got all day. The Court said to let you inspect the premises and . . .'

'And we'll want to inspect them,' Perry Mason interrupted.

'It depends on what you mean by "inspect",' the sheriff said.

'On the contrary,' Mason told him, smiling, 'it depends on what the judge meant by the word "inspect".'

'Well, I don't think you need to be very long here,' the sheriff said.

'That's your interpretation,' Mason told him. 'The Court gave us all this afternoon and all day tomorrow.'

A second car drew up and men carrying mine detectors debouched from the car.

'What's all this?' the sheriff asked.

'The experts who are going to help me inspect the premises,' Mason said.

'The hell they are.'

'That's right,' Mason said, still smiling. 'Many hands make light work, you know, Sheriff, and I take it you'd like to have the inspection over with as soon as possible.'

'What are they going to look for with those things?'

'We're searching for metal,' Mason said, 'metal which may have been buried a foot or so under the surface of the soil.'

'What sort of metal?'

'Any metal.'

The sheriff thought things over. 'You can look,' he said, 'but you can't go digging.'

'We're looking,' Mason said. 'Those things are to help us look.'

'The judge didn't say anything about that. When you look, you're supposed to use your eyes, not any instrument.'

Mason took a magnifying glass from his pockey and said, 'How about this? Can I look through this?'

'Of course, if you want to,' the sheriff said with sarcasm. '*I* didn't find it necessary to use one.'

'It's an instrument,' Mason said.

The sheriff thought that over.

'Of course,' Mason pointed out, 'you have the keys, and if you want to eject us from the premises, why that's fine. Then I'll go into court Monday morning and ask for a further continuance of the case until we have an opportunity to make a reasonably satisfactory inspection of . . .'

'Oh, go ahead,' the sheriff said, and then added grimly, 'after the way you treated me, I don't aim to go out of my way to do anything for you. I'll do what the judge said, and that's all.'

'That's all we expect you to do,' Mason told him.

'As a matter of fact,' the sheriff went on, 'you'll find your attack on me didn't do you any good. People on that jury live in this county and they're taxpayers. I'm popular with the taxpayers.'

'I'm glad to hear it, Sheriff.'

'You start throwing mud at me and those people are going to resent it.'

'I'm quite certain they will.'

'Now, what was the idea throwing dirt at me about that envelope?'

'I wasn't throwing any dirt,' Mason said. 'I was merely trying to clarify your testimony. I think I did that.'

'You sure as hell did,' the sheriff said. 'Come on in.'

They trooped in through the gate which the sheriff locked behind him.

Mason said to the men who carried the mine detectors, 'Over there in that sandy patch, boys. You can begin over there, and then work around the yard over towards the lawn, and then make a swing around by the landing pier over there.

'Paul, you and Della stay with me.'

The sheriff said, 'I don't know what you want to keep fighting this case for. She's guilty. We have evidence we're going to put on that will knock you right out of your chair. If you want to cop a plea you could make a deal with the DA for second degree. He's reasonable about things like that.'

'Are you speaking with authority?' Mason asked.

'Just giving you a friendly tip.'

'Thanks a lot. I'm glad to see you still feel friendly.'

The sheriff lapsed into silence.

Mason, Della Street, Paul Drake, and the sheriff entered the house, walking through the echoing rooms which somehow were still impressed with the silence of death.

'Now in here's the room where it happened,' the sheriff said. 'The bloodstain's still on the floor. They wiped up the blood, but the stain itself will have to be sanded out.'

'Where's the room where the dog was kept?' Mason asked.

'Over here.'

The sheriff opened the door.

Mason regarded the scratches on the inside of the door, said, 'It's your understanding he'd been using this room for the dog for some time?'

'That's right. Whenever he had people coming in he'd put the dog in that room.'

Mason regarded the scratches on the door. 'As you have so aptly pointed out,' he said, 'those scratches are all fresh.'

'That's right. The dog heard a quarrel. He knew his master was in danger, and then he heard the shot. Naturally he wanted to get out to protect his master.'

'Sounds reasonable,' Mason admitted. 'Now, the bullet went clean through the body?'

'Clean through,' the sheriff said, 'and out those french doors.'

'That,' Mason said, is something that interests me. You can't be certain that . . .'

'Well, you're not going to make a red herring out of that, not with *this* jury,' the sheriff said. 'I know the people in this county pretty well. I know six of the people on that jury so I call them by their first names. I know how they react to things in this county.'

'I'm quite certain you do, Sheriff.'

They walked back into the main room.

Mason looked the place over with careful scrutiny, then said,

'Do you happen to remember whether there was a step-ladder around here, Sheriff, a good, tall step-ladder?'

'Good lord,' the sheriff groaned, 'what do you want with a step-ladder?'

Mason pointed to the peaked ceiling. 'I want to examine that little place right up there in the ridgepole.'

'What place?'

'Up there where the beam runs into it. It's a little difficult to see but it . . .'

'Sure enough, there *is* something up there,' the sheriff said, 'but I don't know what difference it could make.'

'It might make a great deal.'

'What do you think is up there?'

'It could be a bullet,' Mason said.

The sheriff regarded him with frowning suspicion, then looked up once more at the all but invisible hole on the right-hand side of the ridgepole at a point where the beams had been cut on an angle to join into the two-by-six which served as a ridgepole and to which the heavy rafters had been attached.

'What would a bullet be doing up there?' the sheriff asked.

'Just resting,' Mason said.

'Yeah,' the sheriff told him, his voice heavy with sarcasm, 'I get it now. Two guys were in here and they wanted to fight a duel, and they turned their backs and walked ten paces, then turned around to fire simultaneously, only Alder fired straight up in the air because that hole's right over where his body was found. The other guy shot him through the heart; so it was s duel and the guy acted in self-defence.'

'Any time you get done having your little fun,' Mason said, 'we'll hunt up a ladder and inspect that hole.'

The sheriff seemed vaguely uneasy as he looked up at the hole. 'I don't think that thing was there when we found the body,' he said.

'Why not?' Mason asked.

'If it had been, we'd have seen it. We looked the room over for bullet holes.'

'Sure,' Mason said, 'you looked the walls over. You didn't look at the ceiling.'

'Well, I don't think it's a bullet hole anyway. I think there's a ladder down in the basement.'

'Let's go get it.'

The sheriff led the way down to the basement. They found a

153

long step-ladder and, after some manoeuvring, managed to get it up the stairs and into the big spacious study.

They erected the step-ladder and the sheriff insisted on his official prerogative of being the first up the ladder.

'Looks like it might be – well, something,' he said, and took a pocket-knife from his pocket and opened the blade.

'Just a minute,' Mason said, 'I want to warn you, Sheriff, that if that's a bullet, the markings on it may be of the greatest importance. You go digging around and scratching it with a knife and you may destroy evidence that would be vitally important to the defendant in this case.'

'Yeah, I know,' the sheriff said, opening the small blade of his knife and thrusting it up in the hole, then moving it back and forth.

'Did you take that down, Della ?' Mason asked.

Della Street said, 'Every word of it.'

'Say, wait a minute,' the sheriff said. 'I'm not giving any reported interviews.'

'You just think you're not,' Mason told him. 'I warned you to leave that bullet alone and preserve the evidence intact. I have my statement and your reply. That's my protection.'

'What protection have I got ?' the sheriff asked angrily.

'You don't need any,' Mason told him. 'You're an officer of the law – but if there's a bullet up there, Sheriff, you're going to have to get on the witness-stand and tell about finding it and getting it out and account for any scratches or mutilations. It may be vitally important to determine what gun fired that bullet.'

'Say, how did *you* know that bullet was up here ?' the sheriff asked.

'I didn't,' Mason said. 'I only surmised that it might be up there. I . . .'

There was a shout from the ground outside the window. Through the open window, a man could be seen running towards the house.

'Now what ?' the sheriff asked angrily, getting down off the step-ladder.

'We found it !' the man shouted, as Mason went to the window. 'We found a gun.'

The sheriff, angrily indignant, strode to the door, opened it and ran down the steps. Mason, Paul Drake and Della Street followed behind.

'Hang it,' the sheriff said, as they hurried across the yard, 'that's what comes of letting your stooges get out here without anyone watching them. They planted a gun and . . .'

'I wouldn't make an accusations, Sheriff,' Mason said.

'Well, it's just all *too* damned opportune,' the sheriff grumbled. The men were grouped around a little hole in the sand.

'There she is,' one of the men said. 'We didn't touch it. When we got a squeal out of the doodle-bug, we just dug down easy-like to see what was down here and as soon as we saw what it was we left it alone.'

The sheriff bent down, scratched around in the sand, then reached down, picked up a sand-covered revolver, held it up in front of him and blew the sand off of it.

'You may want to look on it for fingerprints,' Mason said, 'although it probably won't do you any good. Even when a gun hasn't been buried, there's only small chances of finding any fingerprints on it.'

'I know, I know,' the sheriff said. 'Nevertheless, I've got to see what this is. It looks to me as though this had been planted.'

'Oh, it does, does it ?' Mason said.

'That's right, it does,' the sheriff announced grimly, swinging the cylinder out to the side. 'One exploded cartridge,' he said, '.44-calibre.'

'Now then,' Mason told him, 'you've botched up this case so far. Here's some significant evidence. Let's see what you do with *it*.'

'I don't need any of *your* advice,' the sheriff said angrily.

Mason moved his men over towards the section of beach opposite the french doors. The men put up a rather small-mesh, tilted screen.

Mason, studying the house, mapped out an area. 'Just sift the sand here, boys.'

'Say, what the hell are you looking for now ?' the sheriff asked.

'The fatal bullet,' Mason said.

'Well now, *that's* different. You boys go right ahead, only remember I'm here now and you can't plant a thing.'

The men carefully dug up the light sandy soil, let it sift through the screen.

'Say, there *may* be something to this,' the sheriff said. 'We could have done this, I s'pose. Only it didn't seem there'd be any need of . . . Hey, wait! There it is! There's the bullet!'

The sheriff scrambled forward, retrieved a somewhat battered lead bullet which had faint, reddish discolourations on its point.

155

'Okay, boys,' Mason said cheerfully. 'We can knock off now.'

'Say, what calibre is this?' the sheriff asked.

'I have an idea it's a bullet from this forty-four,' Mason said.

'Look here, if you think I'm going to fall for all this hocus-pocus, you're crazy,' the sheriff stormed. 'I'm not going to monkey with all this red herring mess of planted clues!'

'Well, of course,' Mason said casually, 'you're the one who has the friends on the jury, Sheriff. You're the one who has to run for re-election. If you want to get thoroughly discredited, go right ahead. You've done fine so far.

'Come on, boys. Let's go.'

CHAPTER TWENTY-ONE

Seated in his office, Mason gleefully read the morning newspapers.

Headlines announced: SECOND MURDER WEAPON IN ALDER CASE FOUND, and down below these headlines: UNEXPLAINED BULLET LODGED IN RIDGEPOLE!

'Well,' Della Street said, watching Mason's smile, 'are you going to read it aloud?'

Mason nodded, said, 'I'll give you a few of the highlights here and there. Listen to this one:

'Sheriff Leonard C. Keddie disagreed sharply with ballistic experts. The bullet which was found in the ridgepole was, he insisted, one which had been planted there subsequent to the murder. How, he demanded, could a man be shot through the neck with the fatal bullet going straight up in the air? The bullet, he insisted, could not have come from the gun found under Alder's body.

'On the other hand, Hartley Essex, the ballistics expert employed by the district attorney's office, is equally positive that regardless of how the bullet arrived at its destination it is a bullet fired from Alder's gun. Moreover, he now feels positive the .44 bullet found by searchers is probably the fatal bullet. A small fragment of dried human tissue was till adhering to the bullet when it was found.

'It has been established that the .44 bullet was fired from the gun found buried in the sand. This poses a most embarrassing series of questions for the prosecution. Which bullet killed Alder? If the one in the roof, Alder must have been leaning forward, bent over when the shot was fired.

'On the other hand, if the .44 bullet was the fatal one, the whole theory of the prosecution needs revising. Even if someone stood in front of George S. Alder and fired the fatal bullet with the forty-four, how did the bullet from Alder's own gun, found *under his body*, get into the ridgepole?

'It is also to be remembered that medical testimony already introduced by the prosecution is to the effect that the fatal bullet was a .38-calibre. It is understood a host of experts are available to the defence, anxious to testify that the hole of an entrance wound made by a bullet is almost always smaller than the calibre of the bullet, due to the elasticity of the human skin, which is pushed far inward before the bullet actually penetrates.

'However, if the prosecution should now change its contention as to the calibre of the fatal bullet, the defence will have a field day with the experts who have already testified.

'The .38-calibre double action unquestionably belonged to George S. Alder in his lifetime. Not only had Alder secured a permit to carry a gun and mentioned the numbers of this gun in his application for such a permit, but records show that the weapon was sold to George S. Alder some two years ago, and Alder's signature appears on the record of firearms sold.

'Hartley Essex, the ballistics expert, explained that bullets, in going through a human body, are quite frequently deflected by bones and will do extraordinary things; but obviously he is not too happy about the position of the bullet in the Alder case, or about the prospect of facing further cross-examination by Perry Mason when the case reopens Monday morning.

'Dr Jackson B. Hilt, the autopsy surgeon who performed the post-mortem on the body of the deceased, insists that the course of the bullet, while ranging slightly upward, showed no evidence that the bullet had been deflected by bony structures of the body. Assuming that the man was standing in an approximately upright position at the time the fatal shot was fired, the course of the bullet was such that the point of exit was approximately two inches higher than the wound of entrance. Yet a plumb line suspended from the place where the bullet was found shows that it points almost directly to the centre of the bloodstain which indicates the position where the body was lying.

'Further statements were not forthcoming because District Attorney Claud Gloster clamped the lid down as soon as it appeared that there was an official variance of opinion between the sheriff and the ballistics expert. Shortly after statements were made by these men, they suddenly became as quiet as though a legal muzzle had been clamped over their mouths. When asked for an elaboration of his original statement concerning the bullet, Hartley Essex, the ballistic expert, merely gave a tight-lipped "no comment".

'Sheriff Keddie, obviously restless under the admonition of the district attorney, said, "I'm not going to say another word."

' "Does that mean that you've changed your opinion that the bullets you found were planted ?" he was asked.

' "No, it doesn't," he announced, grimly. "I may be keeping quiet, but I'm not changing my opinions."

'The unexpected developments in the case followed an examination of the premises by Perry Mason, attorney for the defendant, Paul Drake, a private detective employed by him, and several deputies armed with devices designed to detect the presence of metallic substances below the surface of the earth.

'The .44 revolver, when located, was found to be fully loaded, with one empty cartridge case in position under the hammer, indicating that only the one bullet had been discharged from the gun.

'It is, therefore, quite evident that interesting possibilities have been opened up by this somewhat tardy discovery of the fatal bullet, provided it is the fatal bullet.

'It is assumed that Perry Mason may now attempt to show that George S. Alder must have committed suicide, or was the victim of an accidental discharge of his own gun. Despite the fact that Mason's client has insisted she was not on the premises that night, despite circumstantial evidence indicating that this statement is, to put it mildly, subject to some correction, Perry Mason is in the advantageous position of being able to conform his court-room strategy to whichever direction the cat may jump.

'It is assumed by court-room experts who have been following the trial that it will be necessary at some stage of the proceedings for Mason to put his client on the stand, and at that time it is almost certain that she will be forced to change her statement that she was not at the beach city on the night of the murder. Too strong an array of facts and of witnesses have been piled up to enable her to consistently maintain her original position that she did not leave the Monadnock Hotel Apartments where she was living on the night in question.

'However, once having made that concession, the attractive defendant is in a position to go on from there as circumstances may indicate. Inasmuch as these later developments are as much of a surprise to the district attorney as they were to the sheriff, it is obvious that the prosecution finds itself faced with the necessity of anticipating a surprise move on the part of the defence, and since Perry Mason is known as a past master at staging dramatic last-minute surprises, there is no doubt but what the court-room will be crowded Monday morning when Judge Garey resumes the trial of the case of the People of the State of California versus Dorothy Fenner.

'While outwardly everything remains serene, there is court-house gossip to the effect that Claud Gloster, who felt positive he could achieve the triumph of adding Perry Mason's scalp to his belt, is quite obviously unhappy about the failure of the authorities to make a sufficiently careful search of the premises to reveal the bullet hole in the ridgepole, and there are persistent rumours that a strained feeling has come to exist between the district attorney's office and that of the sheriff.

'Sheriff Keddie not only insists that his office did not overlook the bullet in the ridgepole, but demands enlightenment as to how it happened that Perry Mason, who had never been on the premises before, walked into the room, and within a matter of minutes was pointing out a bullet hole which had previously been overlooked by all investigators.

' "How," Sheriff Keddie demanded indignantly. "did Perry Mason know it was there?"

'That probably will be the sixty-four-dollar question which Claud Gloster will hurl at Perry Mason in front of the jury Monday morning.

'But those who have been following the astonishing legal career of Perry Mason point out that hurling questions at Perry Mason in front of a jury is apt to be a dangerous pastime.

'In any event, developments since the Friday adjournment have been such as to change the complexion of the case. Deputies in the county offices who can get away are quietly staking out their claims to reserved seats in the court-room of Judge Garey in anticipation of the Donnybrook Fair which they insist will take place when court convenes Monday morning at ten o'clock.'

Mason folded the newspaper and grinned at Della Street.

'Chief,' she asked, 'how *did* you know that bullet was up there?'

'I didn't.'

'But, as the reporter points out in the newspaper, you entered the room and within a few minutes discovered a bullet hole which had eluded all the investigators!'

'I did for a fact.'

'What were you looking for when you found that bullet hole?'

'The hole made by a bullet.'

'How did you know it was there?'

'Where else could it have been? The sheriff had examined all other places.'

'It was assumed that it had gone out through the french doors.'

'It's dangerous to make such assumptions,' Mason said.

'But how did that bullet get up there?'

Mason grinned, 'I'm not sticking my neck out, Della, but you'll want to be in court Monday morning. I think I now know what happened.'

'Who won't?' she asked, laughingly.

'Won't what?'

'Be in court Monday morning.'

CHAPTER TWENTY-TWO

As court convened on Monday morning even standing space was at a premium.

As Perry Mason entered the court-room, Dorothy Fenner tried in vain to catch his eye, then, managing to catch Della Street's attention, she made a little gesture, a plea for understanding.

Della Street moved over to stand by the defendant as a deputy sheriff moved closer to keep a watchful eye on what was going on.

Mason, preparing for the battle which was to follow, opened his briefcase and spread out papers on the polished mahogany counsel table.

'Miss Street, *can't* you make him understand?' Dorothy Fenner asked tearfully. 'I thought that what I was doing was for the best. I thought I could trap George Alder into making some admission that would help us. I thought I could perhaps get some definite information about Corrine. I don't think Mr Mason appreciates . . .'

Della Street patted her shoulder reassuringly. 'Of course he does, honey. He understands now. But you must understand what it meant to Mr Mason to have his whole plan of defence suddenly blow up in his face. He . . .'

'But please speak to him. *Please* intercede for me. He's so magnificent, so perfectly marvellous, and . . .'

Abruptly there was the sound of motion as the entire court-room rose to its feet and Judge Garey made his entrance from chambers. The bailiff intoned the formula which convened court, and Judge Garey motioned for everyone to be seated.

Della Street leaned close to Dorothy Fenner's ear to whisper, 'I'll tell him, Dorothy. Good luck.'

Judge Garey cast a somewhat disapproving eye over the morbid crowd of thrill-seekers that had jammed the court-room to capacity. Then he announced dryly, and in a voice which indicated he had no intention of permitting his court-room to be turned into a circus sideshow for the benefit of curious spectators, 'Case of People versus Dorothy Fenner. The defendant is in court and the jurors are all present. So stipulated, gentlemen?'

'So stipulated.'

'So stipulated, Your Honour,' Claud Gloster announced, getting to his feet. 'I now have a statement which I wish to make to Court and counsel.'

'Very well, go ahead.'

'There have been certain developments in this case,' Gloster said, 'with which Your Honour is doubtless familiar, inasmuch as they have been featured in a thoroughly deplorable way in the Press.

'In view of the manner in which these developments took place I cannot help but believe that this was a carefully stage-managed procedure on the part of the defence, and I . . .'

'Your Honour, I object,' Mason said, jumping to his feet. 'I demand that the district attorney withdraw that statement and . . .'

'And I am prepared to meet that challenge,' Claud Gloster shouted. 'I am going to prove that this so-called new evidence was planted – by someone.

'It is apparent in the very nature of things that all of this so-called new evidence simply can't be accounted for on any possible theory of what happened there the night of the shooting.

'And if some of this evidence was planted, then it *all* could have been. The prosecution is going to abide by its original theory of the case.'

'Well, gentlemen,' Judge Garey said, 'as far as the Court is concerned, we can't predicate a lot of discussion on so-called new evidence which has been disclosed only in the Press. If there's any new evidence to be disclosed, let's have it.'

'Well, if the Court please,' Gloster said, 'circumstances have developed which are going to make it necessary to make certain corrections in the testimony given by witnesses for the prosecution. It is not a question of inaccuracies, merely a question of certain corrections.'

Mason let the jury see his broad smile. 'Do I understand that the district attorney wishes to recall certain witnesses to make corrections of inaccuracies in their testimony?'

'Now, there is a typical example of the manner in which everything I have said has been systematically distorted during the course of this trial,' Gloster said. 'I specifically stated to the Court that they were *not* inaccuracies.'

'Oh, I beg counsel's pardon,' Mason said. 'Let the record show, then, that the district attorney wishes to recall certain of his witnesses to correct *accuracies* in their testimony.'

Members of the jury smiled. Gloster glared angrily, tried to think of the proper comment, but failed. Judge Garey, frowning, leaned forward to administer a mild rebuke when Mason, again taking the lead, said, 'If the Court please, at this time I once more wish to renew my request that we be told where the dog is. The Court has repeatedly made an order that we are to be told where that dog is and . . .'

'Do I understand that you have not as yet been advised by the prosecution where that dog is?' Judge Garey asked.

'Exactly,' Mason said.

'Mr District Attorney,' the judge said ominously, 'I have repeatedly advised you that the defence are to be told where this dog is to be located.'

'There was some discussion about the matter Friday morning,'

Gloster said, 'and I – well, I confess, Your Honour, that new things kept coming up so fast that the matter entirely slipped my mind.'

'I think the Court will bear with me and the record will show that on Friday I *repeatedly* asked the district attorney for the address where this dog could be found, and I think the record will show that the district attorney stated he would refuse to give me that address because that would tip me off to the location of a witness the district attorney intended to call.'

'No such thing,' Gloster said.

'And,' Mason went on, 'I asked the district attorney if he was afraid I would be able to convince the witness that she should tell an untruth and he said, "No," and I then asked if he was afraid that I would get her to tell the truth.'

'I remember that interchange very well,' Judge Garey said.

Gloster became suddenly silent.

'Now, then,' Mason went on, 'every time that I have tried to find out about this dog, every time I've come reasonably close to finding out, I have been met with this same subterfuge, this changing of the subject, this avoiding of the issues.'

Judge Garey said, 'Well, we are going to find out where that dog is now before there is any other move made in this case.'

'Where is he?' Mason asked.

Gloster said, 'If the Court please, he is with a witness by the name of Carmen Monterrey and I submit that it would be improper to disclose the address of that witness.'

'I want to find out about that dog,' Mason said. 'I either want to know where the dog is, or I'll call Carmen Monterrey and ask her a question about the dog.'

'What's the address? Where's the dog?' Judge Garey asked Gloster.

'Frankly, Your Honour, I don't know. I only know that Carmen Monterrey has been subpoenaed and she is waiting in the ante-room of my office, and . . .'

'Let's get her here, then,' Mason said.

'I submit, Your Honour . . .'

'I'm inclined to agree with counsel for the defence,' Judge Garey said. 'Let's get her in here. Let's put an end once and for all to this business of having the Court make an order that the defence is to be given certain information only to have it appear day after day that the information has been withheld.'

'Your Honour, I think that is an unjust criticism,' Gloster said.

'Don't you remember my making the order ?'

'Well . . . yes.'

'And isn't it a fact that you have failed to comply with it ?'

'Well, I don't think so, Your Honour. I . . .'

'Then how does it happen that counsel for the defence is able to stand up here and ask again for the address at which this dog is being kept and state that he doesn't know where it is ?'

Gloster thought that over for a moment, then said, 'Very well, I'll call Carmen Monterrey and we'll get that phase of the case over with. I'll admit recent events caused me to forget about the dog.'

There was an intermission of two or three minutes during which a bailiff was sent to the district attorney's office to bring Carmen Monterrey into the court-room. Then she came forward and was sworn.

Gloster said, 'Your name is Carmen Monterrey ?'

'Yes, sir.'

'Are you acquainted with a dog named Prince, a dog that was held by George S. Alder for the last few months of his life ?'

'Very well. Corrine Lansing got that dog after he had been discharged from a course of Army training. He was still young and a little green, but I carefully trained him so that he became a steady, dependable dog.'

'And you are very much attached to him ?'

'Yes.'

'So that when you heard of the death of George S. Alder you wanted the dog back ?'

'That is right.'

'Purely for sentimental reasons, and not because you wanted to conceal the dog ?'

'That's quite leading, Your Honour,' Mason said.

'It certainly is,' Judge Garey snapped.

'Well, those are the facts. Let's get at them. Let's not waste all our time arguing about this *dog*,' Gloster said. 'All I've been hearing ever since this case started is dog, *dog*, *DOG !*'

'That is right,' Carmen Monterrey said. 'Only because of affection for the dog.'

'And where is the dog now ?'

'I have him in the house where I am living.'

'And where is that ?'

'It is a house that is owned by my aunt at 724½ North Verillion.'

'And the dog is there now ?'

'Yes, sir. I shut the dog up when I came to court. He will be happy to follow my orders to wait there. When I get home he will be glad to see me.'

'Now, then,' Gloster said, 'I take it *that* disposes of the question of the dog. You may step aside, Miss Monterrey.'

'Just a minute,' Mason said' 'I want to cross-examine.'

'Your Honour, that is the vice of this entire procedure. Counsel keeps trying to . . .'

'I certainly am entitled to cross-examine a witness who has been asked questions under oath by the district attorney,' Mason said.

'Well,' Gloster conceded at length, 'only about the dog.'

'That's all I want to ask about.'

'Well,' Gloster said, 'I guess . . . I think the whole thing is irregular.'

'It's irregular because you didn't tell me where the dog was,' Mason said.

Judge Garey banged with his gavel. 'Counsel will refrain from these personal interchanges.'

Mason turned to the witness and said, 'Did the dog have a broken toe-nail. Miss Monterrey? A broken claw?'

'A broken claw? . . . I don't think so.'

'Was the dog limping?'

'No.'

'Was the dog's foot bleeding?'

'Oh, I remember now what you mean. Yes, in the closet the dog scratched so that his foot began bleeding, but it ceased very soon.'

'You're quite fond of the dog?'

'Oh, yes.'

'And the dog is quite fond of you?'

'Yes, indeed.'

'And you were very much attached to Corrine Lansing, were you not?'

'She was my friend, my mistress. I worked for her for years.'

'Now, then,' Mason said, 'when you returned to this city you saw an ad in the paper inserted by George S. Alder, did you not?'

'Your Honour, I object to that,' Gloster said. 'That's not proper cross-examination.'

'I am now showing the bias of the witness,' Mason said. 'The whole question in this case is whether the dog has a broken or torn claw, and this witness has given testimony which is vital on that point.'

'What do you mean, that's the only question in this case?' Gloster said. 'Why, that's the most absurd . . .'

'Just pay attention to what's going to happen,' Mason said, 'and you'll see how it's important. If the Court please, I think this question is very vital, and I want to show the bias of the witness.'

'Go ahead,' Judge Garey ruled, leaning forward so he could listen to better advantage.

'Did you see such an ad?' Mason asked.

'Yes,' she said.

'And you communicated with the person who had inserted that ad and found out it was George S. Alder, did you not?'

'Yes.'

'And,' Mason said, 'George S. Alder told you that it would be very much to your advantage to come and see him, did he not?'

'Well . . . yes.'

'And you did go to see him, did you not?'

She avoided Mason's eyes.

'Remember,' Mason said as she hesitated, 'there are certain things which can be proven.'

'Yes, I went to see him.'

'When you went to see George S. Alder you asked him about a letter which had purportedly been written by Minerva Danby and thrown overboard from Alder's yacht, did you not?'

She was silent for a long time, then finally said, 'Yes.'

'And,' Mason said, pointing his finger at her, 'you went to see George S. Alder on the evening of the third at about the hour of nine o'clock pm, didn't you? Now, just a minute before you answer, Carmen. Remember that your movements can be traced on that night.'

'Yes,' she said.

'And,' Mason said, 'the dog was very glad to see you, wasn't he?'

'Oh, Prince was overjoyed,' she announced, her eyes and voice softening affectionately.

'Exactly,' Mason said. 'And there was no need for Prince to be shut up in the closet. In fact, it was when he heard your voice that he went crazy in the closet and started scratching the door so that Mr Alder had to let him out. Isn't that right?'

'That is right.'

'And the dog almost ate you up in his affection.'

'Yes, indeed.'

'So,' Mason said, 'when you accused George S. Alder of having murdered Corrine Lansing, and an argument ensued, during the course of which George S. Alder drew a gun, Prince protected you against Alder because he had much more affection for you than he had for Alder. He jumped at Alder's gun arm and clamped his teeth around Alder's wrist, didn't he, Carmen?'

'Oh, Your Honour,' Gloster said, 'I . . .'

'You sit down a shut up,' Judge Garey said, without taking his eyes from Carmen Monterrey. 'Look at the witness. You can see the answer to the question in her face.'

'And,' Mason went on, 'that accounted for the triangular tear in George Alder's left coat sleeve, didn't it, Carmen? That's where the dog's teeth caught when he jerked Alder's hand and that's when Alder discharged the gun with the barrel pointed up in the air so that the bullet struck in the ceiling. And that's when you shot him with a .44 revolver which you were carrying in your handbag, isn't it, Miss Monterrey?'

'I . . . I . . . yes,' she said. 'I had to. He tried to kill me.'

Mason turned with a smile towards Gloster and said, 'Perhaps the district attorney has some questions on re-direct examination. I think the Court will now see the importance of that torn claw.'

'I'm frank to confess I don't,' Judge Garey said, 'but I want to find out what this is all about.'

'The answer is very simple,' Mason said. 'The dog hadn't torn a claw loose. The scratches on the inside of the door were not made when the murder was being committed. They were made when he heard the voice of the one person in the world whom he really loved, the voice of the woman who had been his real mistress for years, Carmen Monterrey.

'Alder let him out. The dog was there and the dog sprang to hold the wrist of George Alder when he tried to kill Carmen Monterrey. She shot him, and I'm satisfied that she shot him in self-defence. George Alder fell forward on his face and Carmen Monterrey was in a panic. She realised she had killed the man, and then she suddenly realised that the presence of the dog would be the most incriminating fact against her, so she put the dog back in the closet. *She was the only person on earth who could have put that dog back in the closet after George Alder was dead.* But the dog had stepped in the pool of Alder's blood and enough blood adhered to the hairs on the inside of his feet so that when he heard her leaving and scratched again to get out, there were blood smears on the door. *That's* how the blood got on the door.

'I think Carmen Monterrey will presently tell us that she took her gun out and buried it, and then she searched the desk until she found the letter which was contained in the bottle, and then she left the premises..

'Some time later, the defendant came down to see George Alder, and walked in just as Alder had instructed her to do. I think there, Your Honour, you have your murder case.'

Judge Garey looked at the crestfallen district attorney. 'I think so too, Mr Mason,' he said. 'Court is going to take a thirty-minute adjournment while we investigate this matter outside of the presence of the jury. Then they will return and the district attorney can take such action as he sees fit.'

CHAPTER TWENTY-THREE

Mason, Della Street and Paul Drake sat in the lawyer's office. A container held a bottle of champagne and three champagne glasses were filled to the brim on Mason's desk.

'Here's to crime,' Mason said.

'And the greatest lawyer of them all,' Drake amended. 'Boy, the way you managed to keep Gloster all tied up in knots, even when he had you on the run as far as the facts were concerned, is one of the greatest pieces of court-room technique I've ever seen.'

Mason grinned and said, 'I kept prodding him about telling me about the location of the dog and then I'd let him change the subject or I'd change the subject myself so he'd forget all about it, until Judge Garey really thought there was something sinister about the whole business.'

'How did you know that – well, how did you know what had happened?' Drake asked.

'Believe it or not,' Mason said, 'and while I'm not going to ever tell anyone else, I'm actually kicking myself that I didn't know a lot sooner. First let's take the fundamental facts into consideration. George Alder had been carrying on a ruthless enterprise. His half sister, Corrine, on the verge of a nervous breakdown, disagreed with him. He had some papers for her to sign and he flew to South America.

'She didn't sign the papers. He reported that she refused to sign them, refused to see him after that, and disappeared, presumably a suicide in a fit of despondency.

168

'But who knows? Her body was never recovered. She simply vanished.

'With the disappearance of Corrine Lansing, George's hands were tied for seven years unless he could find some pretty good circumstantial evidence that Corrine Lansing had actually died, and prove the time and the place when she died and show that there had been a dead body which presumably was hers.

'At this point that mysterious letter from Minerva Danby enters the picture. It had been written by a woman. It accused George Alder of murder. It put Alder in a very embarrassing position. Obviously if he'd murdered Minerva Danby he must have done it to have kept Corrine Lansing from officially coming to life.

'He made the mistake of confiding in Dorley H. Alder. He may not have shown Dorley the letter, but he told him enough about what was in it so that Dorley realised the implications and the possibilities.

'If there was no trace whatever of Corrine, then Alder's hands were tied for seven years. If they could introduce evidence, even circumstantial evidence, which indicated she had been killed, then the situation would be entirely different – and if she had been confined to that institution and had been burned to death in the fire which ensued, the whole legal situation would have been simplified for both George Alder and Dorley Alder. The trouble was that the letter which gave the evidence that would simplify the case for George Alder also virtually accused him of murder, which tied his hands. But Dorley Alder was under no such moral restraint. Naturally he wanted to see the letter made public.

'So it was entirely natural that he would talk to Dorothy Fenner about it, to see if she had any inkling about the contents of the letter or the facts mentioned in it, and it's quite possible that he wanted to use her as a cat's paw in making the letter public.

'George Alder was in a predicament. He didn't dare to destroy the letter because that would have been tantamount to an admission of guilt – and then of course Pete Cadiz knew about the letter and Dorley Alder knew about the letter.

'Then after Dorothy Fenner sneaked into his house, she knew what was in the letter.

'You can see how the coils of circumstantial evidence began to tighten around George Alder – and when I began to realise how he was trapped by circumstances, I began to study the letter more carefully, and when I saw how cunningly it had been constructed for the purpose of putting him in just such a situation, I began to wonder just who had written that letter and why.'

'What do you think of it?' Drake asked.

'I think it's a forgery,' Mason said. 'If you look at the composition carefully you'll realise that the writing is that of a person trying to achieve a dramatic effect, not the terror-stricken composition of a person who is locked in a cabin on a wild ocean and thinks she is about to be murdered. The whole composition of the thing is far too leisurely. It's a good specimen of carefully prepared dramatic writing, of building to a climax. It's not the type of letter a woman would have written while she was in fear of her life.

'Moreover, when we consider the manner in which it was found, we are forced to a realisation that it *must* have been planted. Pete Cadiz had been searching along that high tide line for several days. Then he suddenly found this bottle right where he had been looking all of the time. It's hardly conceivable that he could have overlooked the bottle . . .'

'But suppose it had drifted ashore only the night before.' Drake said.

'Not a chance,' Mason pointed out. 'Remember that Cadiz said he couldn't get into this little bay except when the water was very smooth, and that it was only during periods of high tide and storm that the waves lashed driftwood way up above the normal high tide line on the beach. Yet on this trip he'd been in there for a week combing the high tide line.'

Drake nodded.

'So,' Mason went on, 'we start figuring from there. George Alder would hardly have planted a letter branding himself as a murderer. Who would have done so? It was in the handwriting of a woman. It may even be a good forgery, for all I know, but a woman probably did it. Who?

'The evidence points to one person. Someone who was trying to force George Alder into a defensive position. It *might* have been Corrine, it might have been Dorothy Fenner, but there was a good chance it was Carmen Monterrey, who felt George Alder had murdered Corrine, of whom Carmen was very fond. That last thought opened up possibilities.

'Then I began to think about the dog in the closet, and the blood streaks, just two or three smear tracks on the inside of the closet door, and a couple of blood smudges on the closet floor.

170

'A bleeding foot would have left a whole lot of smudges and smears. Something was wrong with the picture. At first my mind merely registered a vague uneasiness. Then I began to think about it, and it suddenly dawned on me that if the dog had stepped in a pool of blood and *then* been put back in the closet, those bloody smears would be in keeping with the picture – otherwise they simply didn't fit into the pattern of events.

'So then I started thinking about what must have happened in case the dog really had been loose when the shooting took place and been put back in the closet afterwards.

'Then things began to fit into a logical pattern.'

'But why didn't that track show?' Drake asked.

'It did,' Mason said, 'but when the dog got out there was a wild scramble, and the dog splashed through the pool of blood again and the officers simply didn't appreciate the significance of that one track, in view of the fact that other tracks made by the dog in the blood were all over the place.

'Just as soon as you admit that the dog had stepped in that blood, then the deadly significance of the thing becomes apparent. Conceding that Alder was dead, and the dog was out, then *there was only one person on earth who could put that dog back in the closet!*

'Remember that George Alder was left-handed; that there was a triangular tear on the left sleeve of his coat; that his gun had been fired almost straight up in the air, and that he had been killed almost at the same moment he fired his gun because he had pitched forward and his own gun was found underneath his body. You put all those things together and there's only one answer.

'For some time I had been toying with the thought that Alder might have actually murdered Corrine there in South America. He flew to South America. He wanted her to agree to certain matters of policy and she refused. He suddenly realised that not only was she baulking him, but that she stood between him and a fortune. Perhaps there was a choked cry in the night, a splash and that was the end. But whether he murdered her or not, Carmen had learned to believe he had.

'She remained in South America for weeks, trying to find Corrine's body, trying to get some clue. At the end of that time she was convinced that Corrine was dead and that George Alder had committed the murder.

'So Carmen comes back, still running down clues. She goes to the mental hospital at Los Merritos, running down a clue that a

171

person is there who answer's Corrine's description and suffering from amnesia.

'It wasn't Corrine, but the woman attracted Carmen's sympathy. She sent money to the hospital for this woman – and then the hospital burned.

'A few weeks after that the great idea hit Carmen's mind. At the time of Minerva's death officials had dumped whitewash on George Alder. But suppose that case could be made to look like a murder. What was more, suppose it could be tied into Corrine's affairs in some way. Then Alder would be on the defensive and the truth might come out.

'Carmen determined to try it. She managed to get a bottle that had been drifting for months. She forged that letter and looked around for Pete Cadiz. Then she planted the bottle where he'd be certain to see it. *Then* she sat tight to await developments.

'When she saw that ad in the paper, communicated with Box 123J and learned the man at the other end of the line was Alder, she knew she was ready to strike, to boldly accuse him of Corrine's murder.'

Drake looked at Della Street, sighed and said, 'Well, it sounds reasonable enough now, but thank heavens I wasn't the one that was in there trying that case, with a two-timing client and a district attorney who was laying for my scalp, and me with my fingerprints on the canoe.'

'That goes double for me,' Della Street said. 'It should teach Mr Mason not to go around picking up nymphs who make passes at his canoe.'

Mason laughed. 'It would have been all right if only she hadn't left her bath towel with the laundry mark on it.'

'And thereby got caught,' Drake said.

'A mere slip in her plans, a case of negligence on her part,' Mason explained.

Della Street reached for her pencil. 'A good title for the filing jacket, *The Case of the Negligent Nymph*.'

Mason laughed aloud. 'And incidentally, Della, as Corrine's heir, that nymph is going to come into something of a fortune.'

'How come?' Paul Drake asked. 'I thought the money was tied up in a trust and that on Corrine's death the property vested in . . .'

'It's against the policy of the law,' Mason said, 'to permit a murderer to profit by his crime. Therefore, George Alder couldn't have acquired anything through Corrine's death. And while the point so far as Dorley Alder is concerned might be debatable, he has agreed to a compromise which will give Dorothy Fenner a very comfortable fortune – although I think I should give her a spanking along with it.'

Paul Drake raised his glass, caught Della Street's eye. 'And here's a toast, Della, to the greatest court-room strategist of them all.'

Della Street got up and touched her glass to Drake's. They solemnly drank the toast.

THE FAMILY 40p
Leslie Waller

Truly great novels about the Mafia are few
and far between. *The Family* is not only
the most recent but one of the very, very best.
The *New York Times* called it "a jumbo
entertainment, full of everything" and drew
attention to the book's shattering
combination of big business, violence, raw
sex, protest and comment on the richest
society in the history of the world. It is a
dramatic and engrossing story that exposes a
new breed of gangster less concerned with
strong-arm tactics than with financial
manipulation. Woods Palmer, chief executive
of America's biggest banking empire,
becomes the pawn in an operation of a naked
ruthless power that only the Mafia's mighty,
complex machine can wield with such
effectiveness and shameless brutality.

KING OIL   30p
Max Catto

The voice of my beloved! he cometh,
Leaping upon the mountains, skipping upon
    the hills.   SONG OF SOLOMON

Frank Dibbler, already a millionaire who
wants to be an oil king and become founder
of a dynasty that will perpetuate his name in
the future industrial America that he
foresees, chooses as his wife the daughter of a
Spanish grandee, taking her on the long
hazardous journey from the genteel pomp of
Seville to the vast, untamed ranch-land of
Texas.

This epic yarn is Max Catto's finest and most
gripping novel.